John Young

Rival Routes from the West to the Ocean and Docks at Montreal

SALZWASSER
VERLAG

John Young

Rival Routes from the West to the Ocean and Docks at Montreal

Reprint of the original, first published in 1859.

1st Edition 2022 | ISBN: 978-3-37512-160-0

Verlag (Publisher): Salzwasser Verlag GmbH, Zeilweg 44, 60439 Frankfurt, Deutschland
Vertretungsberechtigt (Authorized to represent): E. Roepke, Zeilweg 44, 60439 Frankfurt, Deutschland
Druck (Print): Books on Demand GmbH, In de Tarpen 42, 22848 Norderstedt, Deutschland

RIVAL ROUTES FROM THE WEST TO THE OCEAN.

AND

DOCKS AT MONTREAL:

A SERIES OF LETTERS

BY

THE HONORABLE JOHN YOUNG,

IN REPLY TO LETTERS OF "A MERCHANT," WRITTEN BY WILLIAM WORKMAN, ESQ.,

MONTREAL:
SALTER & ROSS, PRINTERS, GREAT ST. JAMES STREET.

1859

RIVAL ROUTES FROM THE WEST TO THE OCEAN, AND DOCKS AT MONTREAL.

To the Editor of the MONTREAL GAZETTE:

SIR,—In concluding my letter to the Harbour Commissioners of the 10th December last, in reference to the Report of Mr. Trautwine on Docks at Montreal and on the comparative merits of the St. Lawrence with other routes from the West, I stated that I did not regret the discussion which had already arisen, and will yet arise, on the merits of the projects of our harbour improvements, and I trust also that "some of the gentlemen of large commercial experience and habits of close observation," who agree with Mr. Trautwine's views, would be induced to support these views before the public, and point out the errors in the opinions expressed in relation to Docks at Point St. Charles, and as to the trade of this port, in the many facts and figures by which these opinions have been supported. The hope thus expressed by me has been realised to some extent by a series of eight letters which appeared during the months of March, April and May, in your journal, over the signature of 'A Merchant,' which are intended as a reply to my letter of 10th December, on "Rival Routes to the Ocean from the West and Docks at Montreal." These letters have since been published in pamphlet form, with a Preface, by William Workman, Esq., dated 28th May last, acknowledging himself as the author.

Mr. Workman states in his preface that he "simply desired to present the question on its own merits, quite free from any personal considerations." However sincere in this desire, Mr. Workman has certainly been most unfortunate in carrying it out, for the letters are remarkable for a bitterness of spirit, and an evident and characteristic anxiety to attack, not only my views on the questions at issue, but my motives and conduct. They are filled with the most reckless and therefore harmless statements, and shew an ignorance of the arguments connected with the questions discussed, which is not a little surprising from such a source. Evidence of this will abundantly appear in the extracts which I shall make in the course of my remarks, and nothing would have been easier than to have replied in a similar spirit.

Mr. Workman deserved it, and no doubt some of his friends and mine may have expected it; but it is not to my taste to indulge in such a style of discussion, and Mr. Workman's best friends regret the most, the temper he has shewn. He may depend upon it, that however much the public may relish an occasional hard hit given to an opponent, it will not do to make ill temper, rash assertions and personal detraction the staple of an argument, especially on such a subject as that under discussion.

The letters, however, have afforded an opportunity, which I am not unwilling to embrace, of bringing those important subjects again under public notice, being satisfied that the more they are examined and discussed, the more will they recommend themselves to men of information and candour.

Between Mr. Workman's views and mine on our geographical position, the natural capability of the St. Lawrence, and the means necessary to attract a large share of that vast Western trade, which now flows in another direction, there is a great difference. Mr. Workman is supported by the sole opinion of Mr. Trautwine, a Civil Engineer from Philadelphia, whose residence in Canada only extended over a period of some two months, who had never been in the Western States, and whose opinions on the St. Lawrence route and of its power to compete for the trade of the Western States and Western Canada, harmonise so completely with the opinions expressed by Mr. Workman, that we are not now left in doubt as to the source of his information, and that Mr. Workman himself is evidently one of the gentlemen of "large commercial experience "and habits of close observation," alluded to by Mr. Trautwine. How far Mr. Workman deserves such praise remains to be seen. In the mean time it is only proper I think for me to say, for the information of parties at a distance, that he has never been engaged in, and has had no experience whatever in the Western trade about which he writes so authoritatively—that his only experience as a merchant has been in the importation and sale of hardware.

In my letter of 10th December I stated that it was *impossible*, with our present means of transport below Oswego, that either the bulk of the products of Canada West or of the Western States could pass below Oswego, for the reason that if they did there were no means of transport from Lower Canada to compete in cheapness with what exists from Oswego and Buffalo to Albany. And with the view of changing this state of things, I held it to be imperatively necessary for Canada to secure an enlargement of the Welland Canal, and a Canal from the St. Lawrence into Lake Champlain, so that vessels of 750 tons could proceed from any of the interior Lake Ports, without breaking bulk, either to Montreal, or on to Lake Champlain,—that this would give to the route of the St. Lawrence a superiority over all other routes from the West, which never could be disturbed, and that the success of our railroad system *depended* on the St. Lawrence route having this superiority, and that without this our railways in Canada would prove ruinous investments. Mr. Workman, in reply to this, says not one single word against the enlargement of the Welland Canal. As to the construction of the Caughnawaga Canal he is perfectly furious, pronouncing that work 'visionary and so obviously absurd,"—"its construction a species of commercial suicide,"—"unjust," &c., &c., and "that no single merchant besides Mr. Young approves of it."

It may be worth while, therefore, to enquire whether Mr. Workman is warranted by facts in making such assertions, as an opportunity will be thus given for bringing under public attention the views entertained by competent parties in relation to this Canal.

And first, as to what has been done by the Montreal Board of Trade, whose action on the subject has been as creditable as it has been consistent.

In 1846, it was suggested by me that the construction of a canal from the St. Lawrence into Lake Champlain was necessary for the success of the St. Lawrence canals; and that without this it was doubtful whether western trade could be attracted down the St. Lawrence below Lake Ontario. Mr. Workman will please remember that this was *two years before the St. Lawrence canals were opened* for general traffic. In the spring of 1847, I, in company with Mr. Barrett, Civil Engineer, and a man of great professional ability (since deceased), walked from Caughnawaga to St. Johns, and satisfied ourselves that there were no engineering difficulties to encounter in construction. The public became interested in the project, and a petition, numerously

signed by the citizens generally was presented to the Government, praying for a survey. This was granted; and in October 1847, J. B. Mills, a gentleman of much practical talent in his profession, was named by the Government to survey the same. Early in 1848 he did so; and in a valuable report, recommended a line from St. Johns to Caughnawaga, with the Lake Champlain level. In this Report Mr. Mills states—"It seems to me that, "with reference to this enterprise, the direct in- "terest of Montreal to give every facility and "aid to its prosecution upon that route and lo- "cation that will best serve the prominent con- "considerations and interests which have in- "duced its proposition." Mr. Mills again says —" Can the Government expect to get a revenue "from the existing improvements of the St. Law- "rence, depending only and alone upon "the business of Canada, sufficient to pay "the interest of cost of said works, to- "gether with the annual expenses of supervision "and maintenance." Mr. Mills also gives an extract, in support of this work, from a Report to the Provincial Government in 1833, which states —"It is in the power of the Canadian Govern- "ment to say in what direction the people (of "the north west) shall go to market It is ge- "nerally known among commercial men in "North America, that the portion of the United "States called New England is rapidly becom- "ing a manufacturing country; and I believe it "would be impossible now (in 1833) to estimate "the extent of commercial intercourse which "will take place between the West and New "England, as all estimates of the advancement "and productive power of the north-western "States, even relating to periods and times al- "ready past, have proved themselves to be ridi- "culous failures."

The Board of Trade, in April 1848, asked the Government for copies of the Report and plans as made by Mr. Mills, "for the construction of a "canal from the St. Lawrence into Lake Cham- "plain, in the neighbourhood of Caughnawaga." In July, 1848, a valuable memorial was presented to the Government, which set so fully set forth the great objects of the work, and is so clear in its statements, that, emanating, as it does, from a gentleman so universally esteemed in this city and throughout Canada, it cannot fail to be of interest to the public : —

The Memorial of the Montreal Board of Trade Humbly Sheweth,—

That your memorialists have for some time been deeply impressed with the desirableness of connecting the waters of the St. Lawrence with Lake Champlain by means of a Canal. The commercial advantages which would result from such an undertaking are numerous and highly important.

1stly. By means of such a canal Provisions and Breadstuffs, which are at present imported into the non-producing States of Massachusetts, New Hampshire, Vermont and Connecticut from the West by the route of the Erie Canal, would undoubtedly be brought by the St. Lawrence, the superior cheapness of such a route being such as to defy competition ; so that thus not only a transit trade of considerable magnitude would be secured, but a new and valuable market would be opened for the productions of this Province.

2ndly. That such a canal would prove of immense advantage to the lumber districts on the Ottawa and its tributaries, inasmuch as it would open up a new and permanent market for timber, besides bringing into play the water power so largely available on all the streams for the manufacture of wood stuffs adapted for a Southern market.

3rdly. That it would be the means of completing the chain of water communication from the Upper Lakes by the St. Lawrence to New York, and thus materially assist, under the system of free navigation contemplated, in rendering that river the great thoroughfare to the ocean of the produce of Western Canada and the Western States of America.

4thly. The Financial results which would accrue from such a canal would be of the greatest advantage to the Government, if its effects would be, as it is justly anticipated, to increase incalculably the traffic in the St. Lawrence, by the power it would place in our hands of competing successfully with the Erie Canal, the tolls arising from the Provincial Canals could not fail to be largely increased, and the public revenue proportionately augmented.

5thly. The canal in question will prove of great advantage to the city of Montreal, not only by the direct trade it would be the means of opening up, but by the growth in wealth by a population resident in her rear, which, by natural necessity, would resort to her market for supplies. By the contemporaneous completion of the Portland Railroad, Montreal would also become the centre of three great routes to the ocean, a situation most favorable for the growth and concentration of commerce.

Lastly. A canal connecting the waters of the St. Lawrence and Lake Champlain would have the effect of neutralizing in a great measure the present contemplated railroad from Ogdensburgh, which otherwise would draw the traffic of the St. Lawrence at a point above all our Public Works, thereby inflicting a serious loss on our revenue, but an incalculable injury on the interests of the Lower Province.

Your memorialists are also aware that representations on the subject of such a canal were made last year by a number of the citizens of Montreal, and that according to the prayer of their petition Your Excellency was pleased to direct a survey of a line for the proposed canal, commencing at the St. Lawrence side, at or near the village of Caughnawaga.

It appears to your memorialists expedient, under any circumstances, before deciding the line of the proposed canal, that the country lying between Longueuil and Laprairie should also be surveyed, so that the final preference be given to that line which, after minute investigation and consideration of all the interests involved, shall be deemed to possess a preponderance of advantages in its favor.

Your memorialists cannot help regarding the selection of the terminus of such a canal, in the construction of which a vast expenditure must be incurred, and any mistake regarding which may be looked upon as irremediable, as a matter of the very highest importance, and not to be decided on without the utmost deliberation and the examination of competent and unbiassed authorities.

Wherefore your memorialists would humbly pray your Excellency, as a preliminary step, to direct the survey of the country lying been Longueuil and Laprairie, so that a choice of a route for the proposed canal may subsequently be made, after a due balancing of the various circumstances *pro.* and *con.* affecting each line respectively.

And your &c , &c.

(Signed,)

PETER McGILL,
Prest. M. B. of T.

F. A. Wilson,
Secretary.

Montreal, 26th July, 1848.

Such a memorial is worthy of being preserved as part of the history of the proposed Canal, and will be possessed of much greater interest, years hence, when the advantages to be derived from the work shall have been demonstrated by actual experience.

A word or two as to the action of the Legislature on this subject.

In 1849 a bill was carried through Parliament authorising a Company to construct this canal. In the same year a meeting of American gentlemen interested in the subject met at Troy, who authorised a survey by Mr. Claxton, C.E.—and the same year also a Convention was held at Saratoga Springs, where delegates from Canada and different parts of the United States were present, who heartily approved of the utility and necessity of the work. In the same year the Hon. J. B. Robinson brought the subject before Government in his Public Works Report. In Public Works Report of 1851 the Hon. Mr. Killaly and myself alluded to the work, and recommended its immediate construction. In 1853 a special general meeting of the Board of Trade was called in reference to this Canal, and the meeting was *unanimous* as to its necessity. The point of departure from the St. Lawrence was not discussed : while some of the members expressed a desire to have its location so that the Ocean and Western vessel might meet at the same place,—yet, all felt that the point of departure was a matter for Engineers to decide. On this point Thomas Ryan, Esq., (a gentleman who has uniformly and from the first taken an active part in promoting this work,) expressed the feeling of the majority in making the following remarks :— "That the expression of '*the* Canal' he had not "liked, but on a suggestion this had been "changed to '*a Canal.*' This had shown him "the willingness of Mr. Young to meet the views "of the meeting. He did not doubt that such "a Canal as that proposed, if contiguous to the "city, would be of great importance, at *the* "*same time he should be sorry to see any such sel-* "*fishness shewn as would aggrandise the city at* "*the expense of the country.* The city would "extend itself widely, and in a few years a mile "or two one way or the other would make no "great difference with the terminus. But still "the Board would do its best to prevent a wrong "location. He had heard of wrong locations, "and while he would not say that the interests "of Montreal should defeat the clear reports of "approved Engineers, he thought that in the "event of there being two or three different re- "ports, the interes's of the city should come in "and have their weight."

I shall continue this subject in my next letter.

Your Obdt. Servt.

JOHN YOUNG.

Montreal, 23rd June, 1859.

LETTER NO. 2.

To the Editor of the MONTREAL GAZETTE :

SIR,—In continuation of my last letter, I beg to remark that, in 1853, the House of Assembly passed a resolution recommending the construction of a canal into Lake Champlain by a vote of 37 to 6.

In the Annual Report of the Board of Trade in 1855, the whole subject is discussed at length, and its bearing on trade pointed out. It is there stated—"With such a canal, it appears to us "that the immense trade that *is now* diverted "away from this city, by Oswego and other "United States' lake ports, would be brought "to our very doors, and deposited with us as a

"central point for re-distribution, either to the "United States, to the lower ports, or to Great "Britain, as circumstances might require."— Again, in September, 1855, at a general and very full meeting of the Board of Trade, on the subject of connecting the Georgian Bay with the Ottawa by canal, it is stated in the Report— "That, with reference to the immense trade "which must always be carried on, and which "is rapidly increasing, between the Eastern "States and New York, on the one hand, and "the regions on the Western Lakes on the other, "your Committee conceive that the time is near "at hand when increased canal accommodation "must be provided. Whether this can be most "effectually accomplished by the enlargement "of the present Welland Canal, the construction "of a canal to connect the Georgian Bay with "Lake Ontario *via* Lake Simcoe, or by connect- "ing that Bay with Montreal by the improve- "ment of the Ottawa River, is a question which "can only be decided by an actual survey of the "several routes. But whatever route may be "chosen, your committee believe that *an outlet* "*to Lake Champlain is indispensable*, by the "projected canal between that lake and the "River St. Lawrence, a subject which has been "so frequently adverted to by the Council and "approved of by the Board of Trade."

In the Annual Report of 1856, the Board again advert to the great and growing diversion of trade from the St. Lawrence, and gave facts to show the necessity of a canal into Lake Champlain. In 1857, the subject is again forcibly alluded to at length, and the Report concludes by stating "that the most urgent demands "ought to be made on the Government in refer- "ence to connecting the waters of Lake Cham- "plain, and for enlarging the Welland Canal, "*as imperatively called for*, whatever outlets in "the lakes may hereafter be formed, and inas- "much as works of such magnitude involve "long delay in construction, it is of the first im- "portance that no time should be lost." I have deemed it necessary to give these short extracts from the proceeding: of the Board of Trade and of the citizens of Montreal, by which, and by other facts, the public will be able to judge how far Mr. Workman is correct in making it appear that the project of uniting the waters of Lake Champlain with the St. Lawrence is "visionary," and "has absurdity on its very face"—"a wild scheme," "unsupported," &c. I shall now proceed to show *that it is necessary for the public interests that the work should be constructed at whatever point or place whereby the general interest of the country can be best promoted.*

A minute of the Executive Council, dated 18th October, 1854, states that in the Report of the Chief Commissioner of Public Works, stating that in consequence of petitions from various localities in Upper and Lower Canada for the construction of a canal to connect the St. Lawrence with Lake Champlain,—that by the vote on 6th April, 1859, of the Legislative Assembly, as well as by the petition of the Montreal Board of Trade requesting that a survey be made of said canal,—that he had carefully perused said petitions and resolution,—that a survey was made in 1847 at the request of certain individuals, who contemplate constructing a canal as a private enterprise ; but that such survey was confined to a particular line, with its terminus at Caughnawaga, and that, from the great importance of the subject, a new survey should be made, &c.

This survey was entrusted to John B. Jarvis, a civil engineer of New York, who reported strongly in favour of the work, and recommended a line direct from Caughnawaga to St. Johns, with a navigable feeder from the Beauharnois Canal.

After receipt by the Government of Mr. Jarvis's Report, an opportunity was afforded of obtaining the opinion of Captain N. B. Swift, a Civil Engineer of great eminence, and who for some years had been Chief Engineer to the State of Massachusetts. Mr. Swift had before him Reports of John B. Mills, John B. Jarvis, E. B. Tracy, and S. Gamble, but did not concur with Mr. Jarvis in feeding the Canal at Caughnawaga from the St. Lawrence at the Beauharnois Canal, and dwelt at considerable length on the various lines proposed, and concluded by stating that " the cost would not exceed $2,086,000,—and I " have no hesitation whatever in expressing the " opinion that the proper line for the proposed " Canal is from St. Johns to Caughnawaga on " the route known as the Champlain level ; in " other words, that the Canal should be supplied " with water from Lake Champlain, as recom- " mended by Mr. Mills." In 1855 and in 1856, Samuel B. Gamble also run several lines, which resulted in a strong recommendation of the line from Caughnawaga to St. Johns. T. C. Clarke, Esq., also reported on the subject, giving the same opinion.

The Honble. Messrs. Lemieux and H. H. Killaly, in their Public Works Report of 1856, state " That after attentively examining into the res- " pective merits of the several lines—some six or " seven in number—and the arguments of the " Engineers thereon, the undersigned are deci- " dedly led to the conclusion that the only con- " trast or comparison necessary to dwell on, is, " that between the ' Beauharnois line' having the " Beauharnois Canal as a feeder with its branch " to Caughnawaga, as recommended by Mr. Jar- " vis ; and the Caughnawaga line having Lake " Champlain for its supply, represented by " Messrs. Mills, Swift and Gamble, as the one to " be preferred, are deserving of the deepest con- " sideration, containing, as they do, a vast " amount of valuable statistics, and a number of " important and ingenious tables. *After a pa- " tient and mature consideration of the entire, the " undersigned are of opinion that the line follow- " ing the Chambly Canal and then crossing to Lake " St. Louis, is that which would combine and afford " in the greatest degree, all the advantages contem- " plated from this improvement.*" And again, " *The absolute necessity for this connecting link in " the chain of the immense Inland Navigation " through this Province and the United States be- " comes more and more apparent every succeeding " year.*" Now, I was not wedded to any particular point for the divergence of this Canal from the St. Lawrence. In 1851, in a letter to a Committee named by the Electors of Montreal, I stated that, as regards the Canal to connect Lake Champlain with the Saint Lawrence, "I shall be prepared to consider " impartially the reasons which may be ad- " duced in favor of the several routes suggest- " ed. Only one route has yet been surveyed " (from Lake St. Louis), and until comparative " surveys are made of other routes, and the merits " of each duly weighed, I shall defer expressing " a definite opinion as to the best point of depar- " ture from the St. Lawrence."

With these facts, I now leave it to the public to judge how far Mr. Workman is justified in writing that " You should also bear in mind " that you may search in vain for a single Mon- " treal merchant, besides himself, who approves " of the Caughnawaga Canal project " " Mr. " Young, by the influence he wields as a large " produce dealer through certain parties who " are members of the Board of Trade, has suc- " ceeded, if I mistake not, in having his Caugh- " nawaga Canal approved of, or favorably notic- " ed." In point of fact, the Board of Trade, while they have laboured to direct Government and public attention to the necessity of *a Canal, have never expressed, or have been called on to express, an opinion as to site,* or on the numerous surveys made since 1854. So that Mr. Workman is once more mistaken.

His assertion, as to the influence brought to bear upon his fellow merchants, scarcely deserves notice, were it not that it affords another proof, amongst many offered in his letters, of his readiness to impute the lowest motives. It might have struck Mr. Workman that "certain members" of the Board of Trade might have acted from conviction or a sense of duty, and not from the influence wielded by a large produce dealer.

But here again Mr. Workman is mistaken as to the facts, for there is not a member of the Board of Trade who will state that I ever used any such influence, or even solicited a vote, at the Board of Trade.

In so far as an expression of opinion, or arguments in favour of such a canal, are likely to influence my fellow merchants or fellow citizens, Mr. Workman will not find fault. He seems in one place to be almost convinced himself that for the Province at large the Caughnawaga Canal might perhaps be beneficial. He says :— " For " whatever may be said in favour of construct- " ing a canal at Caughnawaga, as a means of " adding to the revenue of our other canals above " that point, yet its construction by any " sound thinking *Montreal Merchant* must be " regarded as carrying absurdity on its very face " as in fact the most aggravated species of com- " mercial suicide."

Mr. Workman does not say in direct terms that the canal would benefit the Province, but he evidently leans to the maxim which is quite prevalent enough, and which one would not have expected in such a quarter, that local and not general interests should control the location of such a work.

But he goes further, and gives another reason against the canal :—The St. Lawrence and Lake " Champlain are already united by two excellent " railways ; that with these means of communi- " cation, coupled with the more circuitous route " of the Chambly Canal, he does not see that " any insuperable obstacles exist to the most " extensive commerce between the two points in " question."

Mr. Workman says—." It will be evident to any " unprejudiced mind, that along with the Caugh- " nawaga Canal must spring up a rival to the

" port of Montreal—a bleeder, rather than a feed- " er—at Caughnawaga."

" That the proposed Caughnawaga Canal " would injure the trade of Montreal, and divert " from, rather than draw produce to, Mr. Young's " docks."

" Unite these two points" [the St. Lawrence and Lake Champlain] " and a British bottom in " the great Western carrying trade would be as " rare as a woodcock in summer, or a swallow in " winter."

" But although a large majority of the mer- " chants and inhabitants of Montreal, from the " very absurdity of Mr. Young's projects, have " hitherto regarded them more as harmless " ' will o'-the-wisps' than as actual realities, there " is danger in carrying this apathy too far."

These are grave assertions, and require to be answered. In my next letter I shall have occasion to examine fully the merits of Mr. Workman's two excellent railways, as a means of competing with the canals and railways of the State of New York. But in proof that we have now no means of such competition below Lake Ontario, let me direct public attention to the returns of the trade for 1858, when a larger amount of produce was received at Montreal than in any previous year. Reducing flour to grain, at the rate of five bushels for a barrel, the total *exports from* the lake regions in 1858 were considerably in excess of 1856 and 1857.

The average amount in 1856 & 1857
was, in bushels 51,248,510
Amount in 1858 59,872,566

This shows an increase in 1858 of 14 per cent. Now, let us see where this property went, and the *relative* importance of the different ports receiving flour and grain from the lake regions.

I find, from tables prepared by the Buffalo *Commercial Advertiser,* and which I have carefully examined, that of all the grain and flour moving eastward in 1856, '57 & '58, each point as follows received the per centage set opposite its name :—

Locality.	1856.	1857.	1858.
Buffalo..................	45.5	44.8	47.1
Oswego..................	23.5	15.3	19.2
Montreal..............	10.6	11.8	9.2
West. Ter. Buf. & O. RR.	4.6	5.3	6.5
Ogdensburgh.............	4.7	6.9	6.0
West Ter. Pa. C. RR.......	2.5	4.3	4.3
Dunkirk................	2.9	4.4	3.4
Suspension Bridge.........	4.1	2.3	2.0
Cape Vincent..............	1.6	1.9	1.8
Rochester...............	...	...	...

Could any argument be stronger, than that proved by the fact here shown, *that at present,* with all our means in full operation (except the bridge, which I shall show can have no great influence on the result), we had not in 1858, the power to attract more than nine and two-tenths per cent of Western Canadian and Western States trade in grain and flour alone to Montreal—in fact, there is a decline of 2 per cent, while other places had increased ; and is it not trifling with a subject of the gravest possible character for Canada, to pretend, as Mr. Workman does, that the Chambly Canal, and the Champlain and St. Lawrence Railroads from St. Lambert and Caughnawaga, are quite sufficient, and that "with these, no insuperable obstacles exist for the most extensive commerce ?"

I stated in my letter of 10th December that, from Ports in Western Canada *above* the Saint Lawrence Canals, the exports of grain and flour alone to the United States lake ports were *more than equal to the total receipts at Montreal, both by railway and canal, of grain and flour, received from all of the Western States and Western Canada.* Since writing my letter on 10th December, I have the returns for 1858, which again show the same tendency of movement, as will appear from the following table :—

Exports to United States from Upper Canada Ports of Grain and Flour, in bushels.	Total Receipts at Montreal from Western States and Western Canada by Railway and Canal of Grain and Flour, in bushels.
1856..... 6,005,710	4,888,623
1857..... 4,492,968	4,901,461
1858..... 6,171,332	5,619,205

I have from time to time laboured to shew that there are superior water communications to Albany, through the State of New York, from Lake Ontario, than any possessed at present by Canada ; and it has also repeatedly been shewn that this superiority would be still further increased the moment that the enlarged and deepened Erie Canal could be made available. The improvement in Erie Canal navigation *is now a fact.* From Oswego, boats drawing six feet of water can proceed to Albany, and can now carry 1200 barrels instead of 650, and of course at a cheaper rate. The Montreal and Lower Canada merchants have no means of transport by which they can enter into competition with their rivals in the State of New York for the trade of Western Canada, with the Eastern States, and far less for the trade of the Western States with the Eastern States.

I have stated that this is a matter of the grav-est importance to the people of Canada. I have before pointed out the fact, that after deducting cost of management, and of the usual annual repairs of the Welland and St. Lawrence Canals in 1857, there was a loss of $26,584, and that with the interest the loss to the people for these works was $563,980. The result of the account for these works in 1858 stands as follows, as per Public Accounts :—

Gross Revenue Welland Canal.....$208,361.30
Do   do   St. Lawrence Canal. 54,678.70

                    $263,840.00

Expense of Collection and General Repairs :

Welland Canal........$112,330.57
St. Lawrence Canal... 82,680.69

Expense of usual and General Repairs :

Welland..............$ 82,090.12
St Lawrence.......... 16,619.82

                    293,730.50

Expenditure over income for 1858..$ 39,890.50

To which, if we add the interest on cost of these works, say $14,155,206.25, we have a total outlay, beyond income, of $881,202, or $11,222 more than in 1857. Along with this enormous annual loss on our Canals, which has to be met by duties on imports, we have also to pay the interest on unproductive railways. It is because of these annual losses on our Public Works and the interest which has to be paid on unproductive railways, that our duties on imports have to be so high, and not, as Mr. Workman supposes, to "our representatives "who have advocated the true interests of Mon- "treal in obtaining *a wise protection to her home* "*industry.*" *In consequence of which,* and of the probability of a further increase in duties, Mr. Workman thinks the advancement of Montreal is likely to proceed in an ascending ratio. Now, I am one of those "*flighty, free-trade theorists*" who believe that so high a duty as now exists in Canada on imports *is not advantageous,* but that it is *for the interest of all* that the duties should be as light as possible ; and it is because I believe that our rivers, canals and railways *may be made a source of revenue,* instead of being comparatively deserted, and an enormous annual outlay necessary for their support, that I have joined with those who have urged forward the immediate construction of the enlarged Welland Canal, and of a canal into Lake Champlain, with docks at Montreal, and a 20-feet channel, at low water, to Quebec.

In closing this letter I again repeat that the daily transactions and the daily course of trade alike shew that the cost of freight from Lake Ontario to Albany, Boston or New York, through American channels, has been for the last six years, and is this year, *less* by from 15 to 25 cents per barrel than by the route of the St. Lawrence via Montreal to the same points, by any means of transport now existing, or that will exist when the Victoria Bridge is completed, even including the Chambly Canal and Mr. Workman's "two excellent railways." I make this statement before this the largest business community in Canada, in order that it may be contradicted if it is not true, and to allow Mr. Workman the opportunity of bringing his knowledge of Western trade before the public, for the public good. If the statement I here make be true, as I affirm that it is, then it is a fact of the greatest possible consequence, for it must be evident, that so long as that great stream of commerce from the Western States and Canada West finds a cheaper route to the great consuming markets of the Eastern States, by an outlet from the St. Lawrence 150 miles above any part of Lower Canada, it is impossible that the progress of her cities, cut off from the advantages of such interior trade, can be equal to the cities in States of the Union on the Atlantic; and the Government and Legislature of the country incur a deep responsibility, as they have already done, if they longer neglect to take action in a matter which involves a great reduction, or a continuation of heavy taxation to pay interest on canals and railways which are now unproductive, but which may be made remunerative.

I shall continue this subject in my next letter, and am now,

Your obedient Servant,
JOHN YOUNG.

Montreal, 30th June, 1859.

LETTER NO. 3.

To the Editor of the MONTREAL GAZETTE:

SIR,—I think it has been shewn by my last letter, that the connection of the waters of Lake Champlain with those of the St. Lawrence has been considered, both by the merchants and citizens of Montreal, as a work of the greatest importance not merely in reference to Provincial, but to local interests, and that Mr. Workman in characterising it as "a wild scheme unsupported by public opinion," and "as visionary in the extreme," has contradicted all the public action which has been taken on the subject, and of which, he as a merchant and a member of the Board of Trade should have been aware before writing his letters. The public documents, reports and petitions of the Board of Trade, of the Commissioners of Public Works, and orders in Council, already given, may be set against Mr. Workman's rash assertions. Indeed, it would have been easy to accumulate evidence proving that there has been a greater unanimity, on the necessity and importance of such a work, than has existed in respect to any *other projected public improvement, within the last ten years.*

Opinion has varied as to the best site for the work, and the cry of local interest has been industriously raised; but the entire weight of the *scientific* and *professional* authority has approved the site above the Lachine Rapids. No one knows this better than Mr. Workman, but it suited his views in endeavouring to hold me up "to the indignant scowl of impatient public sentiment" to make the statements referred to, which served to conceal the great lack of fact in his letters, and to divert attention from the real points to be discussed. Deeming, therefore the Canal into Lake Champlain to be the basis of that great increase to the trade of Montreal and of our public Canals and Railways, I shall proceed to examine how far Mr. Workman is correct in supposing that the construction of that work would prove detrimental to public interests.

I have already stated that with all our railways and canals, in both sections of the Province, in full operation, and even with the Victoria Bridge completed, property of all kinds destined for the great consuming markets of the Eastern States and New York can be moved to Albany or Troy at least 15 cents per barrel *less* from Lake Ontario, through American channels, than the same property can be moved down the St. Lawrence to the same points *via* Montreal; and that this is the case at present, is proved by the fact, that out of the whole exports from the lake region in 1858, Montreal only received NINE AND TWO-TENTHS PER CENT.

This fact was dwelt on in my letter of 10th December, and is so important to the whole argument that it should have been fairly met by Mr. Workman. It lies at the foundation of the whole question of rival routes. How could Mr. Workman, therefore, spare time for dwelling on the "vanity" of Mr. Young, "the colossean intel-

...ect of Mr. Young," and the numberless personal allusions which are scattered throughout his letters, and neglect to consider the main fact, which in itself is of more interest to the public than Mr. Workman's opinion of my personal character or conduct? Mr. Workman makes little allusion to this leading fact; he never attemps to refute it. But he proceeds to urge, with the statistics before him, that this canal into Lake Champlain *is not required*, and that the existing means of transport to the Eastern States from *Lower Canada are sufficient*. This view is placed before the public by Mr. Workman as follows, bringing in as usual some of his personal allusions, to give force to his argument : —

" Who, in perusing this extatic burst, would ever dream that the two points—the St. Lawrence and Lake Champlain—are already united by two excellent railways, the distance along one of which, from river to lake, is little more than 20 miles, with its terminus opposite the city; and the terminus of the other at the El Dorado of Mr. Young's imagination—Caughnawaga. With these means of communication, coupled with the more circuitous route of the Chambly Canal, it can scarcely be conceded, and especially when the Victoria Bridge is opened, which it will be this year, that any insuperable obstacles exist to the most extensive commerce between the two points in question. But great stress is laid by Mr. Young on the greater cost of transport by railway than of canal. To remove this disparity, which Mr. Young alleges to be sufficient to drive the carrying trade from Canadian waters, he insists on the construction of the Caughnawaga Canal. Let this point be now examined, on the data furnished by Mr. Young himself. In page 15 he set down the actual cost of moving heavy freight at 1½ cents *per ton per mile ;* say for wheat, about 1 cent per bushel, and for flour 3½ cents per barrel. Now for the shortness of the line of rail, and for handling at both ends, allow 50 per cent over Mr. Young's own contract price, this will bring the transport of wheat from the St. Lawrence to Lake Champlain at something under 1½ cents per bushel, and of flour to about 4½ cents per barrel. How much under these rates could the Caughnawaga Canal, including lockage and everything, carry such produce ?"

Mr. Workman would have accomplished something if he had, from my own figures, destroyed my views or established his own, but he has failed to do this, and made use of the *data* given in my letter to establish a conclusion altogether at variance with facts probably within his own knowledge, and certainly within the knowledge of all persons engaged in the trade.

Mr. Workman ought to know that wheat has never been carried by the Champlain and St. Lawrence Railroad Company, from Montreal or from Caughnawaga, at less, on the average, than $1.25 per ton of 2,000 lbs., or say 3½ cents per bushel for wheat and 9 cents for flour. Take the published tariff for grain in car loads from *St. Lambert* to St. Johns, which does not include the ferry rates or cartage, the rate is $1.00 per ton and $1.50 to Rouse's Point. Now, suppose this rate to be reduced to 75 cents per 2,000lbs. to St. Johns, which is 21 miles, the cost is 2½ cents *from St. Lambert*, and Mr. Workman knows that at this rate parties have to load and discharge the cars, which cannot be put down at less than 1½ cents per bush., or in all 3½ cents. To carry grain cheaply, elevators at each end of a road are necessary. Now, suppose one to be in operation on the St. Lambert wharf, (which is impossible) and another at St. Johns, the cost of so handling grain might be reduced to 1 cent per bushel. If we add to this the 2½ cents for railway transport, we have still a charge of 3½ cts. per bushel, equivalent to 9 cents on flour. That is by the road of twenty-one miles from St. Lambert, and of course it would be greater by the roads from Caughnawaga to the Lake and to Rouse's Point of nearly double that distance. Yet Mr. Workman wishes it to be inferred that the transport of wheat from the St. Lawrence to Lake Champlain can now be done at something under 1½ cents per bushel and flour at 4½ cents per barrel, when he knows or ought to have known, that wheat has never been moved for less than 3½ cents (including ferry rates and cost of handling) per bushel, and flour at less than 9 cents to Lake Champlain by the shortest of the railroads he refers to.

Without any very profound or practical knowledge of Western trade, Mr. Workman might at least have obtained the necessary information on this point, before straining the *data* furnished by me to support conclusions so contrary to facts.

Before proceeding to answer Mr. Workman's question, "how much under these rates could the " Caughnawaga Canal, including lockage and " everything, carry such produce," let me state that, from the united testimony of all the engineers who have examined the several routes for this Canal, as well as from the decision of the highest officers of the Government, and from my own judgment, I am free to confess that to place the Canal at any other point than above the Lachine Rapids, would be to subject the trade of the Ottawa Valley and that flowing into the St. Lawrence, destined for the Eastern

States, to a permanent extra cost of transport, for increased lockage, and would go far to impede, if not to defeat, the object of the Canal, and lessen thereby our ability to compete with the routes through the State of New York. That such a result should be probable, may be a matter of regret, but the question is one to be decided upon facts, upon which we cannot shut our eyes, the fact of the existence of the Lachine Rapids, and the equally certain fact that increased lockage and increased distances cause an increase in the cost of transport. Taking these and the various other facts and circumstances of cost, and the course of trade into consideration, the question in my mind to be resolved is, to settle *what is the best point of departure for the Canal, in regard to the general and permanent interests of the trade of the Province?* If there is a choice of points, then what is the best point for the general and permanent interest of the Province. Believing this principle to be correct, I acted upon it when I had the honor to be one of the representatives of the city, in conjunction with my colleagues. When we were taunted by certain Upper Canada members with expenditures of public money for the Victoria Bridge and Light-houses in the Lower St. Lawrence, &c.; we took the broad ground that we did not ask, and never had asked, for the expenditure of public money at Montreal or in Lower Canada, for any work which was not for the general good, and contended that, in building light-houses on the Lower St. Lawrence, thereby lessening insurance, Western Canada was more benefitted, if her imports and exports were greater, than Lower Canada was—that if the ferry rates for transport across the St. Lawrence at Montreal could be reduced one-half by the construction of the Victoria Bridge, the people of Western Canada were as much interested in that work, although constructed at Montreal, as the people of Lower Canada. It was upon this principle also that the Board of Trade, citizens and Harbor Commissioners urged the *public* character of the works in Lake St. Peter, and that the expense thereof should be borne by the Province.

If therefore it is shewn that Caughnawaga is the best point for a canal into Lake Champlain for general interests, the inhabitants of Montreal must be content to extract from its location there all the advantages and benefits which it is in their power to do. To oppose its location there, without being able to show that the decision is erroneous, would not be successful in Parliament, and would be in opposition to principles already recognized and acted on. No Legislature ought to expend public money at *a sacrifice of general public interests*, for the supposed temporary advantage of a particular locality. If Mr. Workman, instead of appealing to the passions and supposed pecuniary interests of a part of the city population, and trying to rouse their indignation against me for advocating these views, had discussed the principle in question, and shewn its fallacy or its inapplicability to the case in dispute, he would have been more creditably and usefully employed.

Let me beg the attention of Mr. Workman, and of the public generally, to the statement of Mr. McAlpine, formerly Engineer of the State of New York, than whom there is no higher authority on such a subject, who declares that with the Welland and Caughnawaga Canals built, even with the whole Erie Canal enlarged, the cost of transport from Chicago to New York, *via* Buffalo, Oswego, Montreal and Caughnawaga, would be in favor of the Montreal route. His figures are as follows:—

First.—From Chicago to New York by the way of the Lake to Buffalo, the Erie Canal, and the Hudson River to New York.

	By sailing vessels.	By steam vessels.
From Chicago to Buffalo, 914 miles Lake navigation, at 2 and 3½ mills.	$1 83	$3.20
From Buffalo to West Troy, 353 miles Canal navigation, at 8 mills.	2.82	2 82
From West Troy to New York, 151 miles River navigation at 3 and 5 mills.	0.45	0.76
Transferring cargo at Buffalo.	0.20	0.20
1418 miles.	$5.30	$6.98

Second.—From Chicago to New York by the way of the Lakes and Welland Canal to Oswego, and thence by the Oswego and Erie Canals and the Hudson River to New York.

	By sailing vessels.	By steam vessels.
From Chicago to Oswego, 1057 miles Lake navigation, 2 and 3½ mills.	$2.11	$3.70
Additional expense on the Welland Canal, 28 miles, 3 mills.	0.8	0.8
From Oswego to West Troy, 202 miles Canal navigation, 8 mills.	1.62	1.62
From West Troy to New York, 151 miles River navigation, 3 and 5 mills.	0.45	0.76
Transferring cargo at Oswego.	0.20	0.20
1410 miles.	$4.46	$6.36

Third.—From Chicago to New York by the way of the Lakes, the Welland, St. Lawrence,

Caughnawaga and Champlain Canals and the Hudson River to New York.

	By sail vessels.	By steam vessels.
From Chicago to New York, 1632 miles, at 2 and 3½ mills	$3.26	$5.71
Additional expenses on the Welland, St. Lawrence, Caughnawaga and Champlain Canals, 167 miles, 3 mills	0.50	0.50
1632 miles	$3.76	$6.21

Fourth.—From Chicago to Montreal by way of the Lakes and River St. Lawrence and the Welland and St. Lawrence Canals.

	By sail vessels.	By steam vessels.
From Chicago to Montreal, 1278 miles, at 2 and 3½ mills	$2.56	$4.47
Additional expense in the St Lawrence and Welland Canals, 75 miles, at 3 mills	0.22	0.22
1278 miles	$2.78	$4.69

Here we have a difference in favour of Montreal, including the Lachine Canal, of $2.52 and $2.29 per ton by sail and steam vessels over Buffalo to New York by Chicago, and $1.68 and $1.67 per ton over Oswego. Again, the the fact is established by those figures that the route by the St. Lawrence, Caughnawaga, and Champlain Canals to New York from Chicago, has a superiority over Buffalo of $1.50 and $0.79 per ton by sailing and steam vessel, and over Oswego of $0.76 and $0.15. Now, a very general fear is expressed, that unless the State of New York enlarges her Champlain Canal of 72 miles, it would be useless for Canada to build the Caughnawaga Canal Let me point out the error of this. I shall hereafter shew that it is not New York which is the great point of distribution for the New England States. That point at present is the terminus of the Erie Canal at West Troy and Albany. It is at these points where the various railways diverge to Boston and throughout New England, and it is at these points also, where the large fleet of sail craft load for various localities. Supposing, therefore, the Champlain Canal, from Whitehall to the Hudson, remains of the same size as now, the cost of taking the property on to the Hudson at Troy, would be as follows:—

Chicago to Whitehall—1415 miles at 2 mills	$2.83
Additional expenses on Welland, St. Lawrence and Caughnawaga Canals—96 miles at 3 mills	0.29
Transferring cargo at Whitehall	0.20
Cost of transport on present Champlain Canal to West Troy—72 miles at 8 mills	0.58
	$3.90

So that the actual cost of each route as far as Troy would stand as follows, without the Whitehall Canal enlarged :

Via Buffalo.	Via Oswego.	Via Caughnawaga.
$4.85	$4.01	$3.90

This greater cheapness by the Caughnawaga route would be still more evident, did we take into consideration the greater rapidity secured by the St. Lawrence route, and the fact that Whitehall and Burlington are both nearer to Boston than Albany. Now it will be well to point out here another fact in conjunction with the above, and which I shall allude to more fully by and bye, when I come to dwell upon the necessity of docks at Montreal.

Mr. Workman dwells at considerable length upon some remarks of mine as to the excellent position in which Montreal would be placed by her bridge, docks, canals, and railways, and seems to ridicule the idea of any property being stored at Montreal, in consequence of the great cost which would be incurred in coming through the Lachine Canal and going back again to Caughnawaga, if the merchant here found it to be his interest to sell the same in the New York or Eastern States' markets.— In reference to this objection, I admit the cost would be something, but Mr. Workman exaggerates the cost, and, he should recollect, that the greater the cost of locking down and locking up property, the stronger is the argument against a canal with its point of departure opposite the city, for the property must be raised to the level of Caughnawaga, before it can reach Lake Champlain. But taking it for granted, that when all of the proposed Canals are completed, that the Government will (as should be done now) treat the same as being only three canals ; that the Welland will be one section, the St. Lawrence canals (or any of them) a second, and the Caughnawaga Canal a third section, and that the rate of toll will be chargeable when either section, or any portion of the same, shall be used. The Lachine Canal will thus be made free for all vessels and property having previously passed thro' a part of the St. Lawrence canals, so that the actual charge upon the transport of property intended to be held in Montreal (from Caughnawaga and back or a distance of 18 miles), would be 5 mills per ton per mile, the ascertained cost of transport at the rate at which Mr. McAlpine's calculations have been made. The actual cost, then, of the various routes from the interior to Troy or Albany on the Hudson, would be as follows :—

14

Via Buffalo.	Via Oswego.	By Lachine Canal to Montreal and back, via Caughnawaga.
$4.85	$4.10	$3.99

But I shall have again to refer to this subject. I have thus shewn, that with the enlarged Welland Canal, property can be placed at Montreal by sailing vessel cheaper by $2.52 per ton than the same property can be placed in New York from Buffalo, and at $1.68 per ton cheaper *at Montreal* than if shipped from Oswego to New York. I have also shewn that if the Caughnawaga Canal is built, a new route will thereby be opened, which will compete successfully with either Oswego or Buffalo, for Western Canadian or Western States trade, even if the canal from Whitehall is not enlarged. Now, I shall defer for a little, taking up the question of how Montreal is to be benefited by the canal at Caughnawaga, to answer an objection made to it by Mr. Workman. He says: "That if the Caughna-"waga Canal was constructed, the transport of "produce for New York would fall into the "hands of United States forwarders exclu-"sively." Does Mr. Workman know that in 1856 the number of Western Canadian vessels which arrived at Oswego *alone* was 1,499, the aggregate tonnage of which was 261,094, manned by 18,471 men—and that in 1858 the arrivals were 1231; number of men 9859, and tonnage 180,439. Now, I ask Mr. Workman, as "a merchant," whether such a fleet of vessels passing through the St. Lawrence Canals, on to Whitehall, (where he admits the Canadian vessel has a right to go)—would not be more advantageous to Canada and Canadian vessel-owners and forwarders than their present route, of sailing across Lake Ontario to Oswego. On the other hand, are not the interests of American forwarders *now* "more exclusively promoted" than would be the case if a route was opened by which imports from, and exports to the United States could be made to pass through our *own Canals and rivers* by a route cheaper and *quicker and with* 140 *miles* less of American canal navigation?

Mr. Workman's next objection against the Caughnawaga Canal is, that our foreign trade would thereby be ruined, but the consideration of this I must defer till my next letter. Meantime

I am, Sir,

Your obedient servant,

JOHN YOUNG.

Montreal, 2nd July, 1859.

LETTER NO. 4.

To the Editor of the MONTREAL GAZETTE:

SIR,—It is from a belief that there can be no subject of greater interest to your readers, than the discussion of questions which have for their object the increase of the trade of the city and of the Province, that I have dwelt at so much length on the objections made by Mr. Workman against the construction of a Canal from the St. Lawrence into Lake Champlain, and to its location at Caughnawaga. I have explained that its location there, is the result of the most patient examination by various Engineers and officers of the Government, and that while I am willing to bow to their decision, and to acknowledge its correctness, I deem it my duty, as a resident of Montreal, to do what I can to shew the advantages that may result to the city, by the location of the canal at Caughnawaga, if we avail ourselves of the great natural position of Montreal as a Sea and Inland Port. I have shewn that when the Victoria Bridge is completed our means of competing with the routes through New York from Lake Ontario will be exhausted, and that with these means, including the Bridge, property can be carried from Lake Ontario to the Hudson, at least 15 cents per barrel less than it can be carried to the same point via Montreal. To stand still and do nothing in such a state of things, and acknowledge ourselves beaten by the State of New York, in the rivalry for the trade of our own country, and of the Western States with the Eastern United States, is, I think, not the part of wisdom, especially when we are told by men the most competent to judge, that we are in possession of a route to those Eastern States, through the St. Lawrence, which may be made superior *than it is possible* to make any other route through the State of New York. Action, therefore, in these works, calculated to develope the local advantages of Montreal for competition with other cities, is as imperative, as it is that the Government of the country should wake up, and construct without further loss of time, those *public works*, by which alone, our unproductive railways and canals *can be made to pay*. If I have dwelt so long on the necessity of the Caughnawaga Canal, it is because I believe that work to be the basis, upon which any success can be built, and therefore it is that I have desired to meet fairly all Mr. Workman's objections. He says :—

"Mr. Young proposes to construct the Caughnawaga Canal with the avowed purpose of facilitating trade between the West and Lake Champlain and the Hudson River. Mr. Young or any other Western produce dealer may think this advantage cheaply gained by the ruin of our foreign trade. But bad as it would be to sacrifice our foreign for an inland trade, this would not be the worst of the case. The American navigation laws are such as to exclude British bottoms from trading in their waters. Who, therefore, would forego the advantage of this choice at Caughnawaga by placing his produce in a British bottom, when he would be obliged to tranship at Caughnawaga in the event of his declining to use Mr. Young's Canal."

Now, the facts upon these points are simply these : By the Navigation Laws of both countries vessels of either country are prohibited from coasting. An American vessel cannot load at a Canadian port and deliver her cargo at a Canadian port, neither can a Canadian vessel load at an American port and deliver her cargo at an American port. American Navigation Laws *do not* "exclude British bottoms from trading in their waters." American vessels load at Toronto alongside of British ships for Oswego, and if the Caughnawaga Canal was made to-morrow, the 1400 Canadian vessels which now arrive in Oswego, would have the right, under the American Navigation Laws, to proceed down the St. Lawrence and deliver their cargoes at Whitehall. As to our canal navigation, we admit New York boats to ascend the Ottawa, through the Grenville Canal ; we admit them also through the Chambly Canal. There is nothing in our laws, however, to make our doing so compulsory,—but it is found to be a matter of interest, to have as many vessels passing through our canals as possible. Neither would we be compelled to allow American vessels to pass through the Caughnawaga Canal, except on the same ground ; nor do I believe that the State of New York would refuse the free navigation of their canals to our vessels, for the same right granted to New York craft, for through freight ; nor that the General Government of the United States would refuse us the right to navigate the Hudson, if, in doing so, the vessel were bound direct from a Canadian, to an American port. Now, as to the "ruin of our foreign trade." Mr. Workman throughout his letters seems to be impressed with the idea, that our foreign trade, is that trade only, which consists of *imports and exports by sea*. I differ from Mr. Workman entirely on this point, and believe that to increase our imports at Montreal from the Western States, and to increase our exports, either of those imports from the Western States or from Canada West, to the New England States, would be to increase our foreign trade at Montreal, *above what it is*, or may be from sea, as effectually, as if the imports were from Britain, France, Spain, or China. And this is exactly what I desire to accomplish by the Point St. Charles Docks, the Caughnawaga and Welland Canals.

Let it be granted for a moment that the great bulk of the trade which might be attracted down the St. Lawrence, through our canals, would go direct through to Lake Champlain and the Hudson. It will not be denied, I suppose, that, if it resulted in $1,000,000 being collected from our canals, over and above what we now collect, that it would be a great benefit to the country. Again, suppose the route by Caughnawaga established as the best, and that it divided the trade with the Erie Canal—collecting those tolls from our own vessels now paid to the State of New York, and also collecting tolls from American vessels on their way to Lake Champlain, in what way, may I ask, would this state of things *injure Montreal*, more than she is now injured, *by that same trade* passing from her, at Oswego and Buffalo, and at other points on Lake Ontario, 200 miles above us. It must be evident to any one, that the trade of Montreal could not be injured by the route through Lake Champlain via Caughnawaga being made superior to all others above it. Suppose there is no enlargement of the harbour, by docks or otherwise, our present means of attracting trade would not in any way *be lessened* by the great stream of Western traffic passing by the way of Caughnawaga, instead of by the way of Oswego and Buffalo. This, surely, must be admitted. Now, my position in reference to this state of things is simply this :—I have shown it to be impossible, with our present means of transport, to attract any considerable part of the trade of Western Canada and the Western States for the Eastern States below Lake Ontario. I have next shown that, to do so, the Welland Canal must be enlarged, and the Caughnawaga Canal built, to enable vessels of 750 tons to navigate the St. Lawrence ; that, with these works, it has been demonstrated that trade will find its cheapest outlet via Caughnawaga to Lake Champlain ; and no one has yet attempted to deny that this will be the result of those works. Then comes the question—How much of this trade can Montreal secure ?—or can she secure any of it ? At present, the port of Montreal does not begin to compare with Oswego, Buffalo, or Albany, as to facilities for storing and handling grain, flour, provisions, &c. Without machinery for doing so, and storehouses close to the water, this is impossible; *and in these respects*, Montreal, as an inland port, is very inferior to those places. By the great water power within our control, and by the construction of docks, we have it in our power to make Montreal *superior* in facilities for receiving, delivering, storing, and holding Western produce to any inland port on the Continent. Again, we have seen that if this can be done (and it has not yet been doubted), property can be brought here, held here, and sent on to the Eastern States, or to New York, *as cheaply* as if it had originally been shipped via Oswego or Buffalo to Albany or Troy.

But Mr. Workman may ask, why should such property come here at all? I reply that Montreal is not only an inland port equal to Oswego or Buffalo for storing, &c., but is superior to these lake ports in having an unlimited supply of water for milling and manufacturing purposes. It is also *a sea port*, accessible at lowest water for ships drawing 20 feet, and is 300 miles nearer Liverpool than New York. Again, New York is 350 miles more distant from Chicago, than Montreal—by the route of Lake Champlain, and even by the shortest route via Oswego the difference in distance is 140 miles in favour of Montreal. Produce then, shipped here would not only be in a position to be sent to Lake Champlain and Boston, the Hudson or New York, but would also be at a point where the State of Maine, and New Brunswick, could be supplied, either during the period of navigation, or in winter, by means of the Victoria Bridge, and where shipments to Great Britain or other countries could be made as advantageously as from New York. As a point of distribution, then, Montreal may be made superior to any other.

The consumption of the State of Maine alone of grain, flour, provisions, &c, is over one million of barrels. The trade of that State is now almost exclusively carried on through New York. The completion of the canals alluded to, and of the Victoria Bridge, would so cheapen inland transport as to enable our railway to Portland and other places in Maine as well as Mr. Workman's two excellent railways to compete successfully with any other route, but which cannot be done now with profit to the railways.

Mr. Workman, who seems to understand so little of the matter in question, must admit, that it would enable the merchants of Montreal to make our port a great commercial depot for Western produce at all seasons of the year, for on the termination of navigation produce of all kinds could be shipped in winter by railroad, as produce is now carried from Oswego and Buffalo in the same season, and by a much less distance. This state of things, however, cannot be even hoped for, unless docks be constructed. Now this matter of docks at Montreal, is one about which there has been so much discussion, that it may be well for me briefly to state what action has been taken by the Harbor Commissioners,—the Board of Trade and citizens on the subject.

When the remarkable success which attended the operations for deepening Lake St. Peter became evident, it was perceived that the increased size of the ships coming to the port would soon render necessary greater space in the harbor for their accommodation. Impressed with this conviction, I brought the subject before the Commissioners in a letter dated 7th Jan., 1852, when Messrs. Keefer and Gzowski were authorised to examine into the best means of providing ample accommodation for ships drawing 17 feet water; and these gentlemen were also instructed to examine *"particularly* the ground "lying between the foot of the Current "St. Mary and the Lachine Canal at or "near the St. Gabriel Lock, with the "view of ascertaining the possibility of "constructing a ship-canal to connect these "points, and thus afford the means of building "on both sides." These instructions were written by me, and shew, that long before Mr. Workman had become interested in the Craig-street scheme, I had brought it up for consideration. Messrs. Gzowski and Keefer reported on 23rd January, 1853, in favor of docks at Point St. Charles. Up to that time this location had not been noticed, so that Mr. Workman honors me too highly in making me the "projector" of that enterprise. On the 23rd of September, by resolution of the Commissioners, I laid before them a Report on the necessity of increased harbor accommodation, "and not to delay making such pro-"vision until a *pressure* for it should arise," and "that this was the more necessary, from the fac "that there is now abundant evidence to shew "that it is practicable to make a ship-channe "between our harbor and the sea, twenty fee "deep at low water,' and that such vessels as the "*Sarah'* and '*Water Lily*,' of 900 and 1000 tons

" burthen, will prove to be the minimum size of " the regular traders, and that the number will " increase from year to year." I concluded a long paper on the subject by stating " that a " very large extension of the present wharfage " accommodation should be made in the direction " of Hochelaga Bay, and that this point must " become a large shipping place for timber and " lumber of all kinds," but that the extension of the wharfage accommodation to the East in no way detracts from the necessity of docks. I was compelled, by a careful examination of the subject, to abandon the Craig-street scheme, and to approve of the Point St. Charles project. My Report was referred to the Board of Trade and to the public for discussion, but the suggestion did not excite much public interest On the 17th April, 1857, the subject was again brought before the Harbor Commissioners in a Report which urged action as to increased accommodation by docks, and the following resolution was passed :

" That in view of the augmenting trade of the Port, and of the proximate completion of the 20 feet Channel in Lake St. Peter, the Board are of opinion that the time has arrived for taking into consideration the question of increasing the capacity of the Harbour; and that, in order to attract public attention to the subject, and to elicit an expression of public opinion, the Report this day handed in by Mr. Young be published, and the plans of Docks, prepared by Mr. Forsyth, be left for public inspection in the Merchants' Exchange "

A general meeting of the Board of Trade was called by advertisement, as usual, to consider the above, at which meeting it was resolved :—

" That the Council of the Board be instructed to suggest to the Harbour Commissioners the propriety of placing the whole subject of Harbour enlargement before two or more qualified Engineers, to obtain estimates, and an opinion as to the place where increased accommodation can be secured at the least cost and with the greatest facilities to the commerce of the Port.'

It will be seen by this resolution, that it was *at the instance and suggestion of the merchants of Montreal, called specially for the purpose, that the Harbour Commissioners were induced to place the whole subject of Harbour enlargement before two or more qualified Engineers.*

The Engineers selected were Messrs. Childe, McAlpine and Kirkwood. These gentlemen, after much deliberation and consideration of the subject, reported at length, and concluded as follows:—

" The conclusions to which the Board have arrived may be briefly stated as follows:

" 1st. That the natural advantages of the route between the western interior and the sea-board

by the way of the St. Lawrence are sufficient to warrant the expenditures which have been made, and also those which are proposed to complete the improvements along that route; and that when thus improved it will present the cheapest mode of communication not only to the seaboard, but also to New England and New York.

" 2nd. That the amount of business which will be drawn to this route by the advantages which it will possess when so improved, will be sufficient to warrant the expenditures necessary in making them.

" 3rd. That the port of Montreal is the proper place for transferring cargoes from the interior to sea-going vessels; and therefore that the Harbour Commissioners are right in their plans for deepening the channel below Montreal so as to allow vessels drawing twenty feet to come to the latter port.

" 4th. That the present harbour facilities of Montreal are entirely inadequate to accommodate the present trade; and that such an increase as may be expected on the completion of the improvements already mentioned, will require a large addition thereto.

" 5th. That the location of an enlarged harbour at Point St. Charles is the best site that can be found at Montreal; and that the facilities which a harbour at this place, upon the plan suggested, will amply accommodate the trade in question; and finally, that in our opinion the improvements in the channel of the St. Lawrence at and near Montreal, and the construction of the proposed harbour, are not local questions but of national importance, by which the final success of the scheme of Canadian public works will be materially influenced."

This Report was adopted by the Harbour Commissioners on the 10th April, 1858, and the following resolution passed :—

" That the Report of the Engineers, Messrs. John Childe, Mr. J. McAlpine, and Jas. P. Kirkwood, on the enlargement of the Harbour of Montreal, be transmitted to the Board of Trade with a request that the same may be taken into consideration at as early a day possible, with the view of eliciting from that body an expression of opinion on the Rport; as to the expediency of further measures being taken to enable the Harbour Commissioners to carry out the recommendation of the Engineers."

At a special general meeting of the Board of Trade, held 28th April, 1858, it was resolved by a vote of 66 to 33 : —

" That this Board hereby tender their thanks to the Harbour Commissioners, for their prompt attention to the important subject of a survey of the various localities, with the view of providing increased accommodation at this port, as suggested in the Resolution of this Board on the 7th July last; and, after a careful examination of the Report, by Messrs. Childe, McAlpine, and Kirkwood, on that part of the subject, the Board concur in opinion with the Harbour Commissioners, that the best site for the improvements alluded to, is that part of the river lying between

B

the foot of the foot of the Canal and the Victoria Bridge.

"That it be an instruction to the Council of this Board to request a conference with the Harbour Commissioners, to consider and decide upon the best course to pursue in bringing the subject of River and Harbour Improvements before the Government."

This, I believe, was the largest meeting of the merchants of Montreal ever held. Mr. Workman was present, but took no part in the discussion. Yet he says that "*the entire public voice is against*" the project, of the Point St. Charles Docks. Before however, alluding to Mr. Trautwine's appointment and reports, it may be well to notice several remarks and insinuations made by Mr. Workman, which would lead the public to believe, that as Chairman of the Harbour Trust, and in the conduct of its business—I have acted independently of my colleagues in the Commission, and without their authority.

Mr. Workman says:—

"This *brochure* appears in the form of a letter by the Hon. John Young to the Harbor Commissioners of Montreal, of which body he is Chairman, and more than the directing genius, since it is notorious that he not only rules over, but over-rules, the majority of his confreres, on every branch of the subject which he now treats."

And again:—

"They should remember that, although Mr. Young is *unsupported* by his co-Harbor Commissioners, he invariably writes and acts with reference to his bold schemes as if his individual action was endorsed by his confreres in office."

Now, I have acted as Chairman of the Harbor Trust for about ten years. In the whole of that time I do not believe there ever was any business transacted without its being brought before the Board. Nor do I remember of *any action on any subject*, or any business done, which had not the unanimous concurrence of the Commissioners, except in one instance. The gentlemen now acting with me and who have acted with me as Commissioners, will bear me out in this statement. This is another instance of Mr. Workman's reckless and unfounded assertion. Again, in reference to the appointment of Engineers Mr. Workman says:—

"Mr. Young is so demented on this one idea of 'rivalry' with New York and the certainty of Montreal diverting from that city the great arterial produce trade of the West, that he cannot patiently listen to any opinion differing from his own. Had Messrs. Childe, Kirkwood and McAlpine done any thing else than placed the route of the St. Lawrence as superior to any other, or deemed it their duty to report strongly in favour of making the improvements at Point St.

Charles, their opinions would have been discarded. The great majority of the citizens felt convinced of this when *Mr. Young selected these gentlemen and brought them here to make the survey.*"

It seems impossible that a gentleman in Mr. Workman's position could sit down and coolly write the above, when, at the time, he must have known that he was making statements for which he had not a shadow of foundation. Of course, the implied insinuation of Mr. Workman is, that in consequence *of my selection* of Messrs. McAlpine, Childe & Kirkwood, these gentlemen reported, not as their own minds dictated, but as I wished them to do. The facts are these:—The Commissioners, after much deliberation, thought it best to send their Secretary, Mr. Clerk, to the United States to form a Board. With him he had a list of the names of nine eminent engineers, among whom were—Latrobe, of Baltimore; Jarvis, Kirkwood, and Laurie, of New York; Swift, Childe, and Bigelow, of Massachusetts; McAlpine, of Illinois, and Clark, of Pennsylvania. The Secretary had instructions to form a Board *of any three* of the above gentlemen who could attend to the business, and it was not till the return of the Secretary to Montreal that either I or the other Commissioners knew who were to compose the Board. I was slightly acquainted with the late Captain Childe, but had never seen either Mr. McAlpine or Mr. Kirkwood previous to their arrival in Montreal. By this statement, the public can judge of Mr. Workman's recklessness in stating that "Mr. Young selected these gentlemen." How far I can be charged with forcing my views on the public, may be judged by the fact, that this Dock question has now been before the public for *seven years*—that on several occasions I have stated that neither I nor the Commissioners had any desire to proceed with it without it commended itself to the merchants of the city, at whose suggestion the Commissioners are now acting, and as to the charge of "not listening to any opinion," the abandonment of the Craig Street scheme for the Point St. Charles project—suggested by Messrs Gzowski and Keefer, ought to satisfy Mr. Workman that in this also he is mistaken.

As the patience of your readers must be well nigh exhausted, I shall resume the consideration of the Dock question in an early number of your paper.

I am your obedient servant,

JOHN YOUNG.

Montreal, July 7th, 1859.

LETTER NO. 5.

To the Editor of the MONTREAL GAZETTE :

Sir,—In closing my last letter on the facts and circumstances connected with the appointment of Messrs. Childe, Kirkwood and McAlpine, to survey and report on the question of Docks and the capability of the St Lawrence to compete with other routes from the West, it was my unpleasant duty to contradict, in the most positive terms, the assertion made by Mr. Workman, that these gentlemen were selected by me and the implied inference that their Report was made to conform with my views on Docks, &c.

Had Mr. Workman carefully considered their Report, he could not but have noticed that it is based upon a series of statistical fac s, none of which have been as yet contradicted ; the conclusions they arrive at, seem to me to be the necessary deductions from the facts and tables brought forward. Now, it is easy enough to insinuate that the Report was not the result of their own investigation,—that it was an endorsation of my views, and simply a sham, and that these eminent individuals were mere puppets. Mr. Workman should have attached himself to the facts, statistics and arguments contained in the Report, and have shewn them if he could, to be erroneous. But he fails to do this ; for to have given an intelligent opinion upon the statistics would have demanded a knowledge of the subject and facts, which are not shewn in Mr. Workman's letters, but which, it is to be hoped, he may exhibit at some future time. Meanwhile, Mr. Workman *can scarcely expect that his simple opinion* should be considered worth so much, as the mass of uncontradicted statistics which are brought forward in the Report, to sustain the conclusions arrived at, by the eminent Engineers mentioned.

As the consideration of interior improvements and docks at Montreal must, ere long, command the attention of the public, I trust it may be deemed a matter of interest to know all the facts connected therewith. In my last letter I pointed out, that it was at the inst nce and by the suggestion of the Montreal Board of Trade, that the subject of increased harbour accommodation was submitted to a Board of Engineers, and it was also in consequence of a conference between the Harbour Commissioners and that Corporation that a Bill, giving the Commissioners the necessary authority to construct docks at whatever place might be deemed best by the Government,

was prepared and introduced into Parliament. It was, however, too late in the session to proceed with the Bill, besides, it was opposed by petition from the residents in the Eastern section of the city. A public meeting was also called to discuss Harbour Improvements, but in consequence of confusion no opinion was elicited. The meeting, however, resulted in the Harbour Commissioners inviting a number of gentlemen interested in the question to a conference with them, and particularly to consider the propriety of surveying and reporting on a new site for docks, which was suggested at the public meeting namely, that passing through the ground belonging to the ladies of the Grey Nunnery, thence across McGill Street, and through the College property, to the Canal. The Harbour Commissioners at once assented to this being done, and not only this, but agreed to open up the whole subject of proposed sites, and invited the Committee to select an Engineer to take the necessary levels, and also *to name a Chief Engineer, to be approved* by the Commissioners. On the 28th June, 1858, the Committee named John C. Trautwine, Esq , of Philadelphia, and on the 30th the Commissioners approved the nomination. A joint letter of instructions was drawn up and signed on the part of the Commissioners and the Committee. Mr. Trautwine reported in October, against the project suggested by the Committee, also against the Vigor Square and Hochelaga projects ; and, although in some respects he thought highly of the St Charles project of Messrs Gzowski and Keefer, and approved of by Messrs. Kirkwood, McAlpine and Childe, yet, he rejected that, for a site he recommended as preferable, running from the front of McGill Street, past and beyond the Wellington Bridge on the Lachine Canal. Mr. Trautwine not only differed with Messrs. Gzowski, Keefer, McAlpine, Kirkwood and Childe, as to the best site for Docks, but denied the power of the St. Lawrence to compete with the routes through the State of New York, and advised the citizens to give up all idea of constructing Docks for years to come.

In my letter to the Harbour Commissioners, after stating Mr. Trautwine's opinions as to the superiority of the New York route over the route through Lower Canada, that the merchants of Montreal were not fit judges of what was requisite to obtain a share in that trade, and that it was useless to make further efforts at present for such an object. I added :—" In such a policy, " I, as a Canadian, and especially as a Lower " Canadian merchant, cannot coincide."

Mr. Workman misquotes these words as being "a rebuke intended to be crushing" to Mr. Trautwine, because " his advice was detrimental to " the success of extravagant dock schemes." The truth is, the words were not used in reference to docks at all, and Mr. Workman knew this, but he could not resist, even at the sacrifice of candour, having a fling " at the individual !," " a " Canadian and Lower Canada merchant whose "absolutism in such matters was trenched upon." Now a word or two in reference to Mr. Trautwine.

Mr. Workman states that " Mr Trautwine was " chosen mutually by Mr. Young and a Committee of citizens." This is not in accordance with facts: neither the Harbour Commissioners nor myself had anything to do with the choosing of Mr. Trautwine. Mr. Workman knows, that by the resolution of 24th May, the Chief Engineer was to be named by the Committee, and the Chairman, in his letter of 28th June, 1858, says:—" The gentleman whose name I have " to submit as the choice of the Committee, &c "

The Harbour Commissioners were desirous to meet the views of the Committee in their selection of an Engineer, and from the great importance of the subject, they had no doubt but that the Committee would name some gentleman of great eminence in his profession. The Commissioners felt that this was the fact, when Mr. Trautwine was stated to be a gentleman " who " had just returned from the survey of a railroad " for the British Government ;" and again, that " as the completion of the work in which he has " been engaged for the British Government will " probably oblige him to visit Europe, &c." Although Mr. Trautwine's name and fame were wholly unknown to me, yet I felt, and I presume the feeling was shared by my colleagues, that Mr. Trautwine must be very eminent, indeed, in his profession, when he an American citizen, was chosen by the British Government The selection thus made by the Committee was at once approved of. Now, I presume, Mr. Workman (to whom, I believe, the Committee were indebted for Mr. Trautwine's name) knows that Mr. Trautwine was never employed by the British Government professionally or otherwise! Mr. Workman, too, tells us repeatedly of Mr. Trautwine being " one of the most eminent Engineers of the day." Will Mr. Workman point out the works of construction which has made Mr. Trautwine thus eminent, and thereby enable the public to judge, how far he is superior to Messrs. Gzowski, Keefer, Childe, McAlpine or Kirkwood.

Again Mr. Workman says :—

" Now this whole question of Point St. Charles Docks narrows itself down to a mere question of confidence Does any one believe that Mr. Young's antecedents on this question, he is the proper party to make choice of an engineer for another survey, and that any engineer acting under such circumstances would inspire public confidence in his decision, let that decision be what it may. If in accordance with Mr. Young's views would the public not laugh? All the parties who have hitherto acted for Mr Young when selected by himself, have always reported all right on his side, but when the public or a second party gets edging in a word the decisions have not been so agreeable to Mr. Young."

The foregoing is another of the characteristic arguments of Mr. Workman. But, to pass by the complimentary and personal part of it, I would ask what is the meaning of the assertion that the question of docks at Point St. Charles narrows itself down into a mere question of confidence ? Is it a question of confidence, or reliance in the professional reputation of Messrs. Childe, McAlpine, and Kirkwood on the one hand, and of Mr. Trautwine on the other ? or confidence in Mr. Workman's opinions and his personal character on the one hand, and in mine on the other ?

Does Mr. Workman mean that the public is to select a site for docks from its confidence in certain men, and to follow their leader without hesitation, " be that decision what it may." Even in such a view, the docks at Point St. Charles might, perhaps, not compare unfavourably with Mr. Trautwine's scheme. For the former, we have the expressed and published opinions of the following competent authorities at least—Messrs Keeler, Gzowski, Childe, McAlpine, and Kirkwood, Engineers ; also of Commander Orlebar, R. N. (now surveying the St. Lawrence) ; for the other, we have Mr. Trautwine and Mr. Workman.

But the question as to the docks is not one of confidence. It is susceptible of the test of argument and discussion ; for whether they should be built at Point St. Charles depends on the question whether Point St. Charles is the best location or not. To settle this question involves many considerations, among which may be mentioned the cost of construction, the accessibility, extent, and convenience of the docks, taken in connection with the existing facilities for transport of property, and the new facilities of warehouses, elevators, &c. Indirectly, this is the question, as to the kind and amount of trade to be attracted to the docks. These questions all admit of discussion, and of difference of opinion, in which even Mr. Workman " gets edging in a word;" and the more discussion the less of confidence will be necessary, for the public will come to understand the question upon *its merits*, and will judge of a scheme, not by the men who advocate it, so much as by the arguments and acts they bring forward. So that Mr. Workman might do well to try another style, and to look less at "antecedents" and more at facts. He may rest assured, however, if his "decisions have not been so agreeable to Mr Young," the public will think him if he can bring any new facts or arguments to bear upon the subject.

Mr. Workman patronises Mr. Shanly, and says—"He is a gentleman of high professional "acquirements, universally esteemed, and the "wonder is that he has consented to interfere in "such a vexed and warped question." Why, then, should Mr. Shanly refuse to take up a question precisely belonging to his profession, and to a gentleman of such high professional attainments? Surely, it cannot be because other active and large-minded "gentlemen of large commercial experience and close observation," have looked into it and settled it, and because Mr. Workman says "the Montreal public won't have it there."

In reference to this gentleman, it is only proper for me to say that, before Messrs. McAlpine, Kirkwood, and Childe were named as a Board, the Harbour Commissioners were unanimous in desiring Mr. Shanly to act, but at that time he could not do so. The Commissioners, therefore, deemed themselves fortunate in having the opportunity of placing the whole subject of docks before Mr. Shanly, and for the first time requesting an opinion as to that site for docks by which the great railroad interests of the country and of the city, can be best promoted, in connection with the interests of the Harbour.

In relation to the Harbour Commissioners, Mr Workman does not hesitate to make disparaging remarks and hints, as if they had allowed themselves to be drawn away by the visionary views of Mr. Young. He more than insinuates he has no confidence in them, and it is worth while to refer to this subject, if for no other purpose, than to shew that Mr. Workman's views are not participated by the whole public, in whose behalf Mr. Workman so often speaks. It is important, too, inasmuch as the power of the Harbour Trust to proceed with the extensive works under their charge, depends much on the confidence the public may have in their general management. On this subject I recommend to Mr. Workman's attention the Petition of his fellow-merchants,

through the Board of Trade, addressed to the three branches of the Legislature in June, 1858, where the question of the Harbour Improvements is ably treated. A few extracts can only be copied:—

"The rapid progress of improvements in the deepening of Lake St. Peter, so successfully conducted by the Harbour Commissioners, whereby vessels of 2,000 tons are now able to ascend the St. Lawrence to this point without transhipment of cargo, renders it absolutely necessary to provide additional Harbour-room, while the constant increase of River Steamers and small craft will, ere long, absorb all the present available space; and as now required of trade, now seeking this point, require provision of a peculiar character, the most urgent necessity exists for at once proceeding with works involving long delay in construction.'

"Your petitioners are not unaware that strenuous efforts are now being made by parties in this city in opposition to the passing of the Bill in question. They (your petitioners) have given full consideration to all the arguments adduced, and the petition presented, and fail to perceive any reason for changing their own long-established views and opinions, as now again expressed upon this subject, or withholding from the Commissioners the required power to act.

"The petition referred to, charges the Commissioners with neglecting the improvement of the present Harbour.

"Your petitioners, on the contrary, are aware that continuous efforts in this direction have been made by the Commissioners, and with the most satisfactory results. It is, however, manifest to those practically acquainted with the subject, that whatever extension or improvement may be effected in the site of the present Harbour, the Foreign and transit trade we desire to attract, can never be there accommodated. Competition with the great depots of American trade necessitates the construction of Inland Docks, with permanent warehouses, elevators, and all the modern appliances for economic handling of property. No such facilities can be secured in the present Harbour site, subject to periodical destruction by ice, nor should the available space in front of the City be prepared to any great extent for large vessels, at enormous expense, when Docks must be constructed in addition; and the constantly increasing number of vessels of light draught frequenting the Port, will much more profitably occupy the present wharves without any serious outlay being required for their accommodation.

"As regards the question of site for new Docks, upon which some difference of opinion exists, your petitioners believe that the Harbour Commissioners have, like ourselves, simply the desire to select whatever locality be, by competent authorities, pronounced the best, irrespective of any other consideration; and as enquiries, investigations, and conferences are now going on upon the subject, your petitioners consider the provision of the Bill, leaving the ultimate decision to His Excellency the Governor-

General in Council, should be entirely satisfactory to all parties.

"In conclusion, your petitioners desire to bear witness to the energy, intelligence, and entire success which have always character zed the proceedings of the Harbour Commissioners in the execution of their important trust, involving great labour without emolument of any kind; they believe that the Commissioners possess the entire confidence of the great body of the Mercantile community, and they, therefore, earnestly pray that this Bill embodying their recommendations, may receive the sanction of your Honorable House.

" And your petitioners will ever pray.

"(Signed)   THOMAS CRAMP,
" Chairman."

Mr. Workman, in page 14 of his pamphlet, " argues as if I overlooked or denied the fact " that New York and the other ports on the sea- " board, *at all seasons of the year, can hold direct* " *intercourse by sea with foreign nations.*" This disparity every candid and impartial mind will acknowledge, with Mr. Trautwine, renders the *supremacy* of Montreal over New York as a great shipping emporium impossible. Now, such supremacy may mean a superiority in number of ships, &c , or in many other things. It depends not alone on having open sea communications all the year round, but on many and most complex considerations. But such a supremacy was not the question; the question was a question of routes of transport from the West, whether the *improved St. Lawrence route* has not the supremacy over the American, but could compete with it,—whether it could not get a large share of the Western trade,—more than our present 9 or 10 per cent. That was the question which Mr. Workman should have argued. But he fails to do this, and shifts the question on the general and very different one, as to the supremacy of the Port of New York.

I have not time to discuss the question of this supremacy just now, but I acknowledge, in the most unequivocal manner, (in order that Mr. Workman may not again represent me as denying) that New York *has* open sea communication all the year round, which Montreal has not.

As bearing on the comparative advantages of the St. Lawrence route to Europe, I should say that it should be borne in mind that it is only ten years since the restrictive laws of Great Britain allowed foreign ships to enter the St. Lawrence; that the entire absence of lights in some parts of the Lower St. Lawrence only tended to increase the bad name of the navigation; that our railway communication with the interior has only been open three years; that our

Canadian canals have never been completed, and cannot be said to be complete, until a canal is opened into Lake Champlain. Nor are there any means of receiving and delivering produce, at our inland and shipping ports, capable of the least comparison with what exists in American ports, and unless we as Canadians are prepared to provide these means, we cannot expect to obtain a share of that trade, which it is in our power to command.

Before considering Mr. Workman's remarks on the coat of Docks, I shall allude to some other statements in my letter, which it were well had been alluded to by him, either to be approved, or to meet with his "crushing rebuke."

It was stated in my letter, (1st. That accord- cording to Mr Trautwine's scheme of docks " a " vessel would require to come out of the docks " stern first, the breadth not being sufficient for " them to turn round." (2) " That for the exten- " sive mill sites and elevators, laid out on the " plan (Mr. Trautwine's) *there is no water*.

3. That all the water that can be spared from the Canal is leased out already. (4) That when the Canals were enlarged, " the present water " space in the Canal would be totally insufficient " to accommodate two-thirds of the present " number of vessels of double capacity."

(5.) That it was *this land* so necessary for Canal purposes, " that Mr. Trautwine proposed to take," in which to " construct his dock for ocean vessels."

These statements, one would have thought, might have been favoured with some remarks *If they are well founded*, then it is Mr. Trautwine's scheme to which Mr. Workman's choice and polite epithets of " visionary" and "obviously absurd," "unjust and inconvenient" "will o' the wisp"and " folly" should be applied. A dock in which a vessel could not turn; mills without water; docks to be built on land imperatively required for our inland navigation. Surely when Mr. Workman entered upon what he calls " this most disagreeable task, *these* were the statements which, to quote his own words, " in justice to " Mr. Trautwine and the commercial interests "of the city demanded a reply" f om some quarter, more especially when, as he says in his preface, " he was so desirous to present the question on " its own merits, *quite free from any personal* " *considerations.*"

But Mr. Workman prudently remains silent on these points.

It is not alone to Docks, however, or the Caugh- nawaga Canal, that Mr. Workman has so great an antipathy. His objections extend to the location of the St. Lawrence itself, and he evidently thinks that a great mistake has been made in locating it where it is. Mr. Workman states that "in addition to the undeniable objections "already referred to as inseparable from our "climate, our *geographical* and *political* rela-"tions, there still remain unnoticed many other "still more convincing arguments against the "possibility of changing, to the extent imagined "by Mr. Young, the current of the Great West-"ern carrying trade, in its progress towards the "best markets for consumption. Of these we "will briefly notice one not previously men-"tioned, and which arises *out of our very exist-*"*ence as a Colony.*"

In this opinion Mr. Workman is quite consistent for in 1849 he wrote, that—

"The killing defect, produced from its extreme northern course, which the great St. Lawrence assumes just as it disembogues into the ocean, only adds to those other insurmountable difficulties, and clearly points out to the eye of common sense the inevitable destiny of the country. Icebound as this great outlet is, for a large portion of the year, the commerce of the country is forced to find a highway through a foreign territory to the ocean, under many disadvantages which nothing but annexation to the United States can remove."

Now it seems to me that, whether the people of Canada should remain subjects of Her Majesty the Queen, or citizens of the United States, it would be equally their duty, whether as Canadian British or Canadian Yankees, to develope and make available to the greatest possible extent—the various advantages—of their position; nor do I believe that the climate of Canada would be any less rigorous under American than under British rule.

I shall resume the consideration of Mr. Workman's objections to the Docks in my next letter.

Your obedient servant,
JOHN YOUNG.

Montreal, 12th July, 1859.

LETTER NO. 6.

To the Editor of the MONTREAL GAZETTE:

SIR,—It will not, I think, now be a matter of wonder to your readers, why Mr. Trautwine should have written so adversely on the St. Lawrence ever being a successful competitor with the State of New York for Western trade, when a gentleman of such large commercial experience as Mr. Workman pointed out to him the "killing defects" of its northern course; the badness of the "climate," "our being a colony,"

&c. These were serious objections, which "nothing but annexation to the United States could remove." But it is a matter of little consequence to enquire into the origin of these desponding views of the St. Lawrence route. The question is rather as to the truth and soundness of the views themselves. Mr. Workman, it will be seen from numerous extracts already quoted, seems to have aimed more at calling names, hoping to damage the motives and conduct of his opponent, than in meeting his arguments and supporting his own views. Had he been addressing the least informed of the electors of the eastern part of the city, and his avowed object been to excite their passions by any means, fair or unfair, as hostile to their interests, he could not have used a more appropriate style of address. Hence, in the remarks I have to make, I am obliged to bring forward, over and over, the pitiable personalities, because the little of argument there is in his letters is mixed up and concealed in a mass of words, intended doubtless to be severe and annoying to myself, but which I should have allowed to pass, were they not so blended as to render it difficult to consider them apart.

I now refer to another instance of this kind, where Mr. Workman seeks to contradict a statement made by Messrs. McAlpine, Kirkwood and Childe, and confirmed by me, that in the average of the last ten years, from 1848 to 1858, the Welland Canal was opened for navigation twenty days earlier, and five days later, than the Erie Canal, and that the St. Lawrence was open to sea five days earlier, and was closed one day later, than the navigation on the Erie Canal.

The tables from which this data was obtained were given in detail from official sources, and if erroneous could have been refuted. But this was too much labour for Mr. Workman, and he prefers to throw a doubt on the whole statement by saying—

"There is, indeed, an amount of illusion in the entire statements of Mr. Young on this head really astonishing in such a treatise. It may, indeed, be true that the Port of Quebec is occasionally open as early as the end of March or beginning of April, but it is equally true that carriages have traversed the St. Lawrence opposite Quebec on solid ice on the 10th of May. Good cannot ensue from such distortions as Mr. Young's pamphlet abounds in on this head, distortions which the recollection or experience of any one engaged in commerce or navigation amply refutes."

The dates in the tables, referred to the first arrivals from sea, in the ten years alluded to, and were taken from the Exchange Register at Quebec. Thinking, however, that the ice bridge may have prevented arrivals from Montreal, and that Mr. Workman might be correct, I procured a copy of the date of the arrivals of steamers from Montreal at Quebec, during the ten years beginning with 1848, and including 1858, and find that the earliest arrival was on the 6th April, and the latest on the 6th May, and that, therefore, my statement is in every respect correct. Mr. Workman in attempting to throw doubt on it—by stating that some time or other carriages traversed the ice on the 10th of May, is, to use his own words, "real'y astonishing," and "good cannot ensue from such distortions."

I sha'l now proceed to examine sundry objecti.ns raised against the Dock project. These however, are so numerous—and my remarks commenting on Mr Trautwine's opinions are so unfairly represented, that I find it difficult to contrast Mr. Workman's opinions with my own, without entering upon the discussion of these at too great a length I shall, however, be as brief as possible. Mr. Workman says :—

"It is well, therefore, that Mr Young has shewn the cloven foot, and proposed the two projects as an entirety since, by that means he has, as he will discover, the entire public voice raised against him. The inhabitants entertain higher hopes of our future, than to believe it is contingent or dependent upon the construction of some 33 miles of Canal nine miles *above* our port, and across a peninsula already traversed by two railways."

Why Mr. Workman should see the " cloven foot" in my statement, that it is by and through the Canal into Lake Champlain alone, that I expect that increase in the trade of Montreal, which will render Docks for the accommodation of the trade necessary It would be difficult to say, for to so fair and candid a mind as that of Mr. Workman's, such an avowal might have commended itself, especially as it gave him an opportunity to refute the statement. It is stated in Mr. Workman's third letter, that if the Canal at Caughnawaga was completed, property would be stored there rather than at Montreal, and he asks : " would any man in his senses, having before " him the above choice of markets (Boston, New " York, &c.), incur the risk and the cost of des- " cendi g, with his produce, rapids or canal to "Montreal ?" Would he not say from this point, " Caughnawaga, I have Boston, New York, &c , " and from these, Liverpool and all Europe."

Again, " if I at re my produce here, I escape the " contingency of eighteeen miles travel—double " canal dues, and all other expenses of moving "up and down. This is the reasoni g and the " course of action which unquestionably any " sane produce merchant would follow.' Therefore Mr. Workman concludes that instead of giving any proper grounds for Mr. Young's strong opinions " that it is by "and through this project alone, that " he expects the trade of Montreal to increase, " or that he still urges the necessity of docks." " The very reverse would be the issue and that " the proposed canal would inju e the trade of " Montreal and *deter from* rather than *draw* pro- "duce to Mr. Young's docks." In reply to this I would observe that notwithstanding " the Chambly Canal and the two excellent railways" which traverse the peninsula between Lake Champlain and the St. Lawrence, *ninety per cent* of all United States and Western Canadian trade passes by routes 200 miles *above* Caughnawaga. How then is it possible for the produce merchant of Lower Canada, sane or insane, ever to be in the position of standing at Caughnawaga or any other place in Lower Canada to " reason upon the advantages offered by the markets of Montreal, Boston, or New York, without other means of transport being provided, than now exist. One of the main points in my letter, was to shew that without water communication from the St. Lawrence by a ship canal, the trade of the West could not come below Oswego. The fact is undoubted, that but a mere fraction does come down the natural outlet below that point. Even Mr. Workman can not deny that fact. It stares us all in the face, and it seems to me to indicate but too clearly, that as the trade has gone for 7 years past it will continue to go in future, unless some such scheme as that I have been urging be adopted for securing a cheaper route to the American sea-board. It remained for Mr. Workman to prove that the Chambly Canal and the two excellent railways" are sufficient and do compete successfully with Oswego, Buffalo, &c., for Western trade, or to point out the errors of Messrs. McAlpine, Kirkwood and Childe's calculations, as to the power of the Caughnawaga Canal to change this state of things ; " in fact to enable Mr. Workman's " sane produce merchant" to stand at Caughnawaga, to reason upon and decide, whether he will take his produce to Montreal, or to Boston, Albany or New York.

But Mr Workman must know that practically,

and as a matter of fact, the "two excellent railways" have not enabled us to compete for the bulk of the Western trade. His figures as to the cost of transport were shown to contradict actual facts, as proved by the existing rates of ferryage and railway transport, *exclusive* of all wharf dues, cartage, &c. The Western trade has continued to be diverted from Montreal : it does not come within 200 miles of it. It is impossible for any " sane" merchant to shut his eyes to that fact. I endeavoured to show, that with the Caughnawaga Canal finished and the Welland Canal enlarged, a different state of things would arise ; and, if proper facilities by docks were created at Montreal, property might be stored there, and yet could be sent to New York, Albany, or Boston, or to any of the interior towns in the Eastern State, as cheap as if that produce had been originally shipped at Buffalo or Oswego; and that a powerful incentive for so storing and holding at Montreal would be offered to the proprieto of such produce, by knowing that at Montreal the expense of storage, &c., would be as low as at Buffalo, Oswego, Albany, New York, or even Caughnawaga.

I have shewn also that produce, when so stored, would be at a point where it could not only be moved by water or by rail to New York, Boston, Albany or Portland, or to all parts of the Eastern States without increase of expense in transport, but could be shipped into the ocean vessel direct to England or other countries, and that the ocean ship, in the cost of transport from Chicago or other interior Ports to Liverpool and other places, via Montreal, would have a margin of $1.73 by sailing vessel and $2.27 by steamers, over the cheapest route from the interior *via* New York This is shewn by Messrs. McAlpine, Kirkwood and Childe, and I invite Mr. Workman to shew the fallacy of the statement.

The comparison of the distance and cost to Liverpool will be as follows :—

	MILES.	COST.	
		By sail.	By steam.
1st. From Chicago to Montreal	1278	$2.78	$4.69
From Montreal to Liverpool by Straits of Belle Isle.	2682	2.68	5.36
Add for Towage on St Lawrence		.30	..
	3960	$5.76	$10.05

		By sail.	By steam.
2nd. From Chicago to New York, via Oswego	1410	$4.46	$6.36
From New York to Liverpool	2980	2.98	5.96
	4390	$7.44	$12.32
Difference in favor of the St. Lawrence route	430	$1.78	$2.27

Mr. Workman again says :—

" What, according to Mr. Young, is generally our relative position to New York for the supply of European markets with Western produce ? Mr. Young says, page 16 :—' Freight at Montreal to ' Liverpool, up to 1854, has generally averaged ' 100 per cent over the rates at New York, so ' that, although the cost of freight from the inte- ' rior to Montreal is less than to New York. yet ' the gain on ocean freights from New York ' brings the choice of routes for export nearly ' to an equality.' *Now is it not clear that if with all the advantages of the superior cheapness which Western produce can be laid down at our own doors, we are subjected to a close and keen competition with New York in our foreign trade, would not that trade be annihilated by a scheme which would cause us to forego these advantages? in other words, if, from our cheaper inland freights, we have so much advantage over American routes as to barely compensate us for the difference of ocean freight against us at New York, would it not destroy this advantage to contract any canal or work that would place the American forwarder on an equal footing with ourselves with their inland freights ?"*

I am here quoted to show, that for nine years, ending in 1854, the ocean freights were 100 per cent higher at Montreal, than at New York, and that the choice of routes for exports are nearly equal, and, Mr. Workman asks,—" *Would it not " destroy this* advantage to construct any canal " or work that would place the American for- " warder on an equal footing with ourselves " with their inland freight." My reply to this is, that it is estimated that the proposed enlargement of the Welland Canal would cheapen transport $1.00 per ton, or 10 cts. per bbl. But, it may be said, that the American route to Oswego will reap the advantage of this equally with Montreal. Very true. But at Oswego—the 750 ton vessel has to discharge into boats one-sixth of this size, while this same vessel may continue on direct to Montreal. The saving which would thus be effected in cost of freight, and in time of transport, would be very considerable, and of course such saving, coupled with the reduction of those heavy charges at Montreal, arising from the want of docks and those facilities which are to be found at Oswego, Buffalo &c., would *increase our power of competition* with

New York, for the export trade by sea. If the St. Lawrence route for export of produce was about equal to the route via New York, with ocean freights 100 per cent higher than at New York, up to 1854, (but since decreasing) it is too plain for argument, that our power of competition for that export trade *would be increased by any canal or work, which reduces inland freight, and which would lessen charges at this port.* What Mr. Workman says about our b ing subjected to a close and keen competition with New York in our own foreign trade, and about our being annihilated, cannot be well founded, unless cheaper inland freights would tend to annihilate our foreign trade.

I really think it must be " clear" to your readers that Mr. Workman does not understand what he is writing about. To prove his views to be correct, and to be well founded, Mr. Workman must be prepared to shew that the enlargement of the Welland Canal, would *not cheapen* but *increa e* cost of transport to Montreal; otherwise there can be no ground for supp sing that our trade would be annihilated by any scheme which had for its object the *increase* of the "superior cheapness" of our inland transport.

Mr. Workman thinks the Caughnawaga Canal an absurdity, a folly, a will o' the wisp scheme, ruinous to Montreal, and pretty plain proof of the insanity of those who support it. On this subject Mr. Workman and myself must agree to differ. But put the Caughnawaga Canal out of the question for a moment, and let us l ok only at one of the "schemes," the enlargement of the Welland Canal. Is it not evident that our power to compete f r the export trade by sea, would be *increased* by the greater cheapness of freight from the interior to Montreal, by the increased *size* of the vessel navigating the interior waters. Would not the Canal also diminish the cost of freight, destined for the *Foreign Market in the United States?* Would the benefit of such increased cheapness be lessened by allowing the same large vessel to proceed to Burlington or Whitehall? Would Canadian vessels be ruined by a voyage some 400 miles longer than to Oswego? Would Montreal be turned into fields, by bringing even were it only another nine per cent of the Western Trade within nine miles of it? Mr. Workman evidently thinks so, and he has a right to enforce his views as energetically as he pleases, but it was scarcely worth his while to attempt to convince the public that any produce merchant that entertained different views could not be of sane mind, but deserving of "crushing rebuke."

Mr. Workman next tells us that he has been carefully perusing "Hunt's Merchants Magazine" to find out the exports from New York, and the result of his labour is the important statement, that a little more than one-fifth of that large accumulation of "produce, which Mr Young " describes as collected at the various ports on " Lakes Erie and Ontario is exported," that "the " other four-fifths are of course either taken for " consumption, or shipped to other foreign markets." It would have been a much more interesting labour for Mr. Workman to find out the amount arriving at tide water on the Hudson, and ascertaining the amount shipped from all the American ports on the Atlantic, east of New York. If he had done so, he would have found that only about *three-eighths* of the cereals arriving at tide water are exported, while five-eighths are consumed. This statement was made by me in 1855, in a letter addressed to the Hon. F. Lemieux, so that Mr. Workman is again mistaken when he says : " That Mr Young loses sight of " the circumstance, that of the entire quantity of " breadstuffs received at New York, but a small " fraction is shipped from New York."

Again Mr. Workman states :—

" It will, therefore, be seen that alike in error is Mr. Young in grouping together the fifty-two millions of bushels, which he gives as the total receipts at the ports of Dunkirk, Buffalo, Suspension Bridge, Rochester, Oswego, Cape Vincent and Ogdensburgh, with a view of shewing that Montreal in obtaining only 10 per cent of *this* grand aggregate, is a great sufferer, or, that any system of docks or canals could materially change this."

My remarks already made will show that Montreal and the country are great sufferers in not receiving more than 10 per cent; and that the proposed "system of docks and canals" will completely change this. Mr. Workman seems to think he is supported in his opinions by a Western miller, who states that

" There is one controlling principle, he says, " which it seems to me Mr. Young, and, indeed " all you Montreal people overlook, which is, " that along all this Erie Canal route there are " multitudes of very important streams which " Western produce has the chance of flowing " into at good consumptive prices, before it needs " to take the last chance of New York. This one ' thing gives our route a great advantage over ' others, even Oswego. Buffalo is undoubtedly ' from its position the very best grain market in " the country, that is, it will *stand* a larger ar- " rival of g ain at one time without breaking " down than any other place."

And Mr. Workman adds that]

"The fifty-two millions of bushels then, which "Mr. Youn: gives as entering the ports of Dun-"kirk, Buffalo, Suspension Bridge, Rochester, Os-"wego, Cape Vincent, and Ogdensburg on their "way to their various destinations (destinations "which want them and must have them for local "consumption), could not be attracted from the "natural *groove* of supply and demand by any sys-"tem of docks at Montreal, New York, or else-"where. The average shipments at New York to "Great Britain and Ireland, and the Continent of "Europe, for the last year, after adding all that "reaches that port from every other route, is, as "will be seen by the above extract, *only about one-*"*fifth of this quantity.*"

The above quotations from the " Western Miller," and Mr. Workman, are in direct contra-diction to what I stated in my letter of 10th December. I then pointed out the error into which Mr. Trautwine had fallen, of taking the receipts at Oswego, Buffalo, &c., as any crite-rion by which a comparison could be made of the probable receipts at Montreal. In my letter of the 10th December it is stated :— "It is true that the estimate of the receipts of "grain and flour at the lake ports in 1856 was "12,000,000 barrels, but I never stated that "grain and flour were *the only articles* received "at Lake ports ; nor did I state that the 12,000,-"000 barrels were received at tide water in that "year. *I knew that a vast amount was distributed* "*along the line of the Canal, before it reached tide* "*water.*" Yet Mr. Workman, with this state-ment before him, drags in his friend, the West-ern Miller, to make it appear that I was " obli-"vious to all such contingencies ;" and that my estimate of the probable receipts at Montreal being equal to five millions of barrels was ridi-culous, inasmuch as that amount was " a supply "more than double that shipped from New York "to the British Isles, *and all Europe*, out of all "the produce that reached New York from the "said 52 000,000 above named, and from every "other quarter, during the same year." In my letter of 10th December, I stated repeatedly, in reference to Mr. Trautwine's deductions of pro-bable receipts at Montreal, that the exports from New York were no criterion by which to judge of the receipts at Montreal ; and that it was not cereals alone to which he should have confined his esti-mates, but that it was " for a share or proportion "of the amount arriving at tide water in the "Hudson," for which Montreal might be a com-petitor ; and that, " as the receipts arriving at "tide water on the Hudson could be conveyed to "the same point, *via* the St. Lawrence, quicker

"and cheaper than they are now taken there, "even when the Erie Canal is enlarged, I claim-"ed that, whether for export or distribution "through the Eastern States, Montreal would "be a better point than Albany." So that it is not alone for what may be exported by sea from New York, but for a proportion of the amount received at tide water at Albany or West Troy, that Montreal may become a competitor. Mr. Workman overlooks all these statements, which are before him in my letter of the 10th December, f r the purpose of shewing " that Mr. Trautwine's very liberal estimate of " 2,666,666 barrels, or two-thirds of the quantity "of wheat and flour exported from our north-"eastern ports," is all that can ever be expected at Montreal, with all our improvements com-pleted as proposed.

If Mr. Workman had fairly met the argument as put by me, it would have better become his position and standing ; but he does not do so. Mr. Trautwine fell into the error, and it was pointed out plainly ; Mr. Workman *repeats* the error without noticing the explanation. As to the amount of increase to the trade to be derived from the completion of the great works referred to, I do not pretend to speak positively. Indeed no one can speak definitely as to probable re-ceipts at Montreal, with docks and other pro-posed facilities in operation. I only again re-peat, what has already been stated, that it is not for what arrives at the Lake Ports, but for a share of what arrives at Albany or Troy on the Hudson, after the whole of the interior of the State of New York is supplied, the Port of Montreal may become a competitor.

The magnitude of the prize aimed at is im-mense. In 1858, the total receipts at tide water were 1,985,142 tons From this, if we deduct 223 568 tons, the gross amount of the products of the forest, agriculture, manufactures, and other articles of the State of New York, we have 1,761,541 tons arriving at the Hudson from the Western States and Western Canada, or equal to *seventeen* million *barrels*, against *something over one million and a half* at Montreal.

If Mr. McAlpine and other Engineers are cor-rect in stating that, with docks and the Welland and Lake Champlain canals completed, Mon-treal can compete with all other routes for this trade, in cheapness and rapidity of movement, not only for holding here and distributing to the Eastern States, but also for export by sea, it becomes a mere matter of opinion, not resting on actual experience, how much of this amount can be attracted here. Mr. Workman may believe with Mr. Trautwine, who is equally well informed on the subject, from an erroneous view of the data furnished, that we could never hope for more than equal to 2,666,666 bbls. My own views would lead me to go far beyond their limit. But whether the quantity be, or be not, greater than the limit mentioned, and no one can pretend to absolute certainty on such a subject, the arguments I have advanced for the execution of the works in question will still hold good. The *amount* of the benefit is uncertain ; the fact of a large increase to our trade is, to my mind, clearly to be expected. Indeed, so far as carefully considered statistics, drawn from the experience of the actual trade of the West for many years, and calculations as to reduction in cost of transport, based on experience and known facts can prove the matter, the necessity of the works has been shewn.

However much merchants may differ as to the point just mentioned, one thing is quite evident our present share in the vast and ever increasing trade of the West is most unsatisfactory I am more and more convinced of this every year. Without the canals and docks we have no reasonable prospect of attracting any considerable part of that great trade which now arrives at tide water on the Hudson. Even our Chambly Canal and Mr. Workman's *"two excellent railways"* and Victoria Bridge will fail to help us. The reason is plain, we shall then have no means of carrying produce via Montreal from Lake Ontario to the Hudson so cheap by 15 to 25 cents per bbl., as it is now carried through the State of New York.

Mr. Workman may lay the blame on Providence, on the location of the St. Lawrence being too far north, on our climate, our geographical position, our political institutions, and it may be "absurdity," "folly," "commercial suicide," "vanity" or "insanity" to differ from him, but "as hard words butter no parsnips" so they do n t convince me that my views really deserve the epithets referred to.

In my letter of the 10th December I went at considerable length into the financial question of the docks, and gave figures to show, that with the Lake St. Pete debt assumed by the Government, it was quite possible for the Harbour Commissioners to go on with the work without increasing harbour dues beyond past rates. I also then stated that it was of the greatest importance to make the charges on shipping and goods coming to the port, as light as possible. And that the most effectual mode of doing this was to provide conveniencies for reducing the present high rates of charges, and by increasing the trade of the port. Moreover, I stated that I would be adverse to proceeding with the docks, without it was first distinctly understood that the Government would proceed with the Welland and Champlain Canals, and the improvement of the rapids of the St. Lawrence. All this seems to me to indicate a considerable degree of caution, yet Mr. Workman says that " In " the entire advocacy of this dock question, at " public meetings, as Harbour Commissioner in " conference with the Committee of citizens, and " as member of the Board of Trade, at the various " meetings of that body, Mr. Young has ever " evinced the same impatience and reckless de- " termination to launch *unconditionally* into the " enormous expenditure which the immediate " construction of his scheme of docks would en- " tail upon our trade."

Hard words again, Mr. Workman, BUT ARE THEY TRUE ?

Again, I stated that the charges at Montreal on property received here from the interior, were equal to 6 cents per bushel, over and above all wharfages, which six cents might be saved if facilities were created in docks by machinery, and otherwise for receiving and delivering property. I gave several tables, by which this was demonstrated. Mr. Workman does not attempt to refute any of these tables, but contents himself with a far more easy mode of argument by stating that

" It is in vain you endeavour to reason with him, and to shew that an increased *servitude* upon the revenue of our port, equal to the burthen of the Point St Charles Docks, must inevitably increase, to a damaging extent, the cost of shipping both flour and wheat in place of lowering it."

Again, Mr. Workman says in reference to our facilitating trade between Chicago and Montreal by branch houses, &c. : —

" And what would be said of any other city adopting such a course—say of the city of New York—should she, for the mere purpose of giving artificial support, or bringing trade to some pet dock scheme, or to the Hudson River, or the Erie Canal, send the young blood and capital of her commerce to some distant city, whether " Chicago, Milwaukie, or *elsewhere*. Truly, this would be a novel mode of benefitting New York, and yet it is precisely Mr. Young's plan for increasing the trade of Montreal."

Mr. Workman is unfortunate again. This was precisely what New York did do. It was to bring the trade to the Hudson River that the merchants and citizens of New York strained every nerve, and at last succeeded in making what is called the "mere ditch," which brought to the Hudson River so enormous a trade as that to which I have referred. The Erie Canal did not come within 145 miles of the city of New York—Chicago and Milwaukie and all the western cities have all built up New York. Every cent saved in transport builds it up, as well as benefits the producer. Mr. Workman's "two excellent railways" prevent his looking at the vast trade which I seek to attract in part to Montreal, not, as Mr Workman, with little candour, says, to disprove the "supremacy" of New York over Montreal, but to take advantage of the natural and, as I believe, the quickest, cheapest, and best route to New York city, to the Eastern States, or to the ocean.

Let the merchants of Montreal look to the matter, and do so as business men, without the "extatic bursts" that Mr. Workman charges me with. The prize is a part of the great trade referred to. My argument is, that Montreal ough to secure, and can secure, a large share of it. I gave long lists of figures and details, which Mr. Workman sneers at, but cannot confute, and scarcely ventures to contradict; and these figures shew that we can get a large part of the trade. Scan these figures, therefore : see if they are erroneous. Remember that if they are correct, and if they establish the views I am urging, then the sooner that energetic action is put forth to carry them into effect the better. It may be useful here to direct your attention to the effects arising from "that ditch' referred to.

The Erie Canal was opened to commerce in 1826, and the result of that work, on the prosperity of New York, may be judged of by an examination of the following Table :—

Population.	Value Real and Personal Estate.	In. value of Real & Personal Estate
1816..95,516	$ 82,074,020	
1826..165,086	107,474,781..Inc. fm '16 to '26..	25 p ct.
1836..270,089	309,500,781..inc. fm '26 to '36..190 p ct.	

Independent of the vast increase in the population of New York in the ten years following the opening up of the Erie Canal, we see that the increase in real and personal estate, as given in for taxes from 1826 to 1836, was 190 per cent. against 25 per cent., the rate of increase for the previous ten years. Again, take Boston, and there is another remarkable instance of the effect of cheapening transport from the interior. In September, 1839, there were only 167 miles of railway in Massachusetts. In August, 1850, there were upwards of 1000 miles completed. In 1830 the value of Real and Personal Estate

was			$ 59,586,000
In 1840	do	do do	94 581,000
In 1850	do	do do	179,525,000

shewing that between 1840 and 1850 there was an increase of 90 per cent., while in the ten preceding years the rate of increase was only 58 per cent.

I give these statements to shew the intimate connection between the growth of sea ports on the Atlantic and such works as tend to facilitate trade with the interior. Similar results are likely, in my opinion, to take place in the population and wealth of Montreal, whenever her advantages as a sea and inland port can be fully developed, the great water power at her command made available, and the route of the St. Lawrence to the interior perfected.

But to return to Mr. Workman's views. He agrees with Mr. Howland in believing that so long as the American Government persist in charging ad valorem duties on imports at their value whence they are brought in the last place, Western States people can never buy at Montreal, and that consequently we cannot compete with New York.

"Mr. Howland said a great deal of truth in a very small space here. Indeed, it is too evident that this one difficulty alone, were there no other, renders it impossible, so long as the two countries remain under different Governments, to attract the carrying trade of the Great West to our Canadian waters in preference to the New York route—and here again Mr. Young's arguments crumble to the ground."

Mr. Workman's views as to the effect of the two countries being under different governments, I shall not stop now to discuss, as a political question, but would state that in former letters, I pointed out that so far as respects the Navigation Laws of the two countries there was no difficulty. In regard to customs' duties, both countries at present collect these on the ad valorem principle,—that is on the value at the place where goods were last purchased. As a merchant I have the right to send goods to Chicago from Cuba, France, Portugal, or any other country, through the St Lawrence direct, or by transhipping here, and such goods, with American Consul's certificate of value, are entered at Chicago on such value, in the same way as if the goods had been landed at New York. In Canada we have exactly the same right of bringing goods through the United States in bond. I am aware that in either case the goods must go direct and that they cannot leave first hands; but in this there is nothing to prevent the greatest scope for direct imports into the Western States in the same way that Upper Canada merchants formerly imported, and now import largely from Great Britain through the United States. If it is found that the St. Lawrence is a cheaper route than via New York, nothing can prevent this being done. Again, the Montreal merchant can import and place his goods in bond, and sell to Western dealers, just as the New York merchant must now do, to Canadian dealers. Even in such a case, is it not clear after all, that the extra duty to be paid by the Western or Canadian dealers buying in bond, is merely the Tariff rate, on the cost of freight and the merchant's profit. I would have thought that all this must have been evident to Mr. Workman and to Mr. Howland, but it seems to have been overlooked.

I must defer further remarks on Mr. Workman's objections till my next letter, and am

Your obedient servant,
JOHN YOUNG.
Montreal, July 20th, 1859.

LETTER NO 7.

To the Editor of the MONTREAL GAZETTE:

SIR,—In continuation of my last letter on Mr. Workman's objections to docks at Point St. Charles, it may be well to allude to a fact which I daresay is not generally known, and especially among the residents of the eastern part of the city, that the scheme of docks to which Mr. Workman and the Committee have given their consent, extends about 1,000 feet further west, than the Point St. Charles scheme. Indeed, about the half of the whole area of Mr. Trautwine's plan is located beyond the Wellington Street bridge over the Lachine Canal. Yet Mr. Workman says—" These men [the committee] "deserve every encouragement; they are battling against an attempt to do what? To " plant the business of our city remote from its " present centre, from the spot which nature "pointed out to its primeval founders, and " which hitherto has been found to answer every "purpose, to turn fields and pasture grounds "into city lots, and city property into fields." Again, Mr. Workman says—" To the population "of the eastern part of the city, the construction " of docks at Point St. Charles would be as fatal " to their interests as would be the building of " the Caughnawaga Canal to the *general interests*

" of the city." Here, we have Mr. Workman stating that he and the Committee deserve every encouragement from the residents of the eastern part of the city, for battling against docks at Point St. Charles, when he gives his assent to a scheme, which is still *further* "from the spot " which Nature pointed out to its primeval "founders' as the great centre. Besides, Mr. Workman is no doubt aware, that by the Point St. Charles project, a space in the river is proposed to be enclosed, which is public property, and " that the 'fields and pasture grounds,' which are to be turned into city lots and city property, are only embraced in Mr. Trautwine's scheme. It is to be presumed Mr. Workman was quite aware of this, but the opportunity of leaving it to be inferred that pecuniary interest was at the bottom of my advocacy of docks at Point St. Charles, was too attractive to be lost. I am, however, confident that Mr. Workman, in his efforts to promote eastern interests, having already given his assent to a scheme of docks so much farther west than any scheme previously reported on, will yet, when he becomes thoroughly conversant with the whole subject, agree to the location at Point St. Charles, should that be found, after the final surveys, to be best adapted for the trade of the port, especially, as he says that—" The Committee, however, not blindly wedded " to any scheme, but anxious to have the ques-" tion settled on amicable grounds, saw much " merit in Mr. Trautwine's plan of docks, and "expressed themselves willing to accept it." Indeed, the readiness with which the Committee yielded their opinions as to the site through the property of the ladies of the Grey Nunnery, shows they were not wedded to any scheme. Mr. Workman says—" At the first projection of " this notable scheme for removing our trade " from its present centre, and for rendering un-"productive the enormous sums expended for "docks, buildings, and other appliances in and "opposite to our present harbour, and for no "other purpose than to increase the value of "property in another locality, it seemed too "ridiculous to attract notice."

Mr. Workman may think the scheme ridiculous; but that circumstance will not make it so, for Mr. Workman may be mistaken, and his zeal to decry my efforts, may have carried him too far. It would serve little purpose to retort upon Mr Workman, the charge of vanity, dogmatism, &c. But surely he ought to be willing to admit that one may differ from his views, and not merit the appellations and insinuations scattered all through his letters.

Mr. Workman's special aim was to excite the residents of the eastern portion of the city against the v ews losiated on by me. It would not be difficult to shew that no one has done more than myself in advocating those measures upon which the growth of the eastern part of the city depends. It will not be denied that the extension of the general trade of the city must benefit all parts of it, and my action in having the harbour limits extended to Hochelaga Bay, and the various works since completed within that limit and still going forward, and which could not have been completed, or acted upon but for my suggestion and action in recommending the Harbour Commissioners to extend the Harbour limits, ought to satisfy even Mr Workman that I have never sought to act in my capacity as Harbour Commissioner, from any sectional predilections. I am not afraid but that my fellow citizens in the eastern part of the city will yet do me full justice in this respect.

I believe that the city will extend itself in the direction of Hochelaga Bay, especially if that locality is made a depot for the shipment and holding of all kinds of timber, a work easily carried out, and for which the place is admirably adapted. Mr. Workman again says :—

"No one, it is presumed, doubts that with money enough *docks could be* constructed at Point St. Charles. It needs not engineering talent to tell us that. But the *Montreal public* (that is to say *Mr. Workman*) won't have them there. They won't consent to a project that will sink our port irretrievably in debt, burthen our trade, and *remove from our present harbour* our Atlantic and sea-going c mmerce, leaving the hay and wood craft in undisturbed possession of our present harbour."

Mr. Workman wrote this when he had before him the following printed memorandum given by the Commissioners to Mr. Trautwine :—

"The Commissioners, therefore, have found it necessary since 1843 to extend their wharfage accommodation, and to make extensive excavations in the harbour, by emoving shoals, widening and extending the entrance to the harbour, &c ,&c. Since that time, wharves in Bonsecour Basin, Monique Street, and Hochelaga Bay, also Victoria Pier, have been constructed ; and such is the rapid increase in steamers trading with various places adjacent to Montreal, and in the local trade generally, that the Commissioners are now constructing a new wharf 300 feet long (which can hereafter be extended), and 100 feet in breadth, in the Bonsecours Basin, and are also constructing a wharf 1600 feet long below the Victoria Pier, as far down as the Military Hospital.

"This will enable them to remove the wood tr de from the Bonsecours and Basins above, to the wharves below the Victoria Pier, and to improve and adapt that space between the Grand Trunk wharf for vessels drawing not over 16 feet at low water. The space lying between the Island Wharf and Victoria Pier will then in no place have a less depth at low water than 12 feet while about half of the whole space can be fitted up for vessels of 16 feet, without any excessive expenditure ; thus affording accommodation for the local trade, for which, from its proximity to the principal market of the city, this part of the harbour has hitherto been, and can most advantageously and conveniently continue to be used. And for vessels of moderate burthen, trading with the Lower Ports and the West Indies, to provide 20 feet of water would, in the opinion of the Commissioners, entail a useless expenditure of a large sum."

From the above it will be seen with what truth Mr. Workman charges the Harbour Commissioners with seeking to remove the trade from our present harbour.

Then, again, observe the following,—" And " yet so far as settling the question of Mr. " Young's determination, to convert Point St. " Charles' fields into city lots, the whole has " been labour in vain." " Where a man's trea-" sure is, there his heart will be also ;" and, " whether pasture grounds, or prejudice in " Mr. Young's case, it is synonymous." Of course, the public are aware that no land whatever is requisite in the Point St. Charles scheme, but the implied insinuation here, is, that I am a proprietor of land adjacent to the proposed docks, and hence my advocacy of the scheme. I have been long aware that there were parties in Montreal, like Mr. Workman, who believed that my advocacy of this project, was dictated by self interest, and to the advancement in value of property, which I was supposed to hold there. I once contradicted this statement in public, and about the same time *I personally explained to Mr. Workman, that I never owned any land whatever at Point St. Charles, nor do I now own one cent's worth on the South bank of the canal, within the limits of the city*, so that when he sought to detract from the value of my exertions and labours, by the above quotation, Mr. Workman knew, while he wrote, that he was making insinuations contrary to facts. If self-interest guided me in my action respecting docks, I might well advocate Mr. Trautwine's plans, which would add immensely to the value of my property, whereas what land I have on the north bank of the canal, would rather be lessened in value, by affording dock accommodation at Point St. Charles.

I alltd; to this matter, because it is time that persons in Mr. Workman's position, should cease to hint at, and to try to get less informed persons to believe, that pecuniary and selfish personal interests, are connected with my advocacy of the public works in question.

Mr. Workman knew better; but he knew also that if he could make the residents in the eastern art of the city believe that I was acting from personal and selfish ends, to add value to my own property, he would injure the effect of my exerti as in favor of Point St. Charles.

The truth is, that the arguments in favour of Point St. Charles would not be in the least weaker if I owned £150,000 of real estate in that vicinity, instead of not owning a farthing's worth. But to answer arguments is one thing and to impute selfish views another. Mr. Workman chose the easier if not the more honorable course. Mr. Workman occupies half of one of his letters by a critique on the number of Drawbridges proposed to be placed over Mr. Trautwine's Dock, the merits of which can be judged of by the following:—

"Now without disturbing Mr. Young's calcu-"lations let us simply ask,—if a project having "fourteen great thoroughfares' to and from it "would obatruet in Common Street 10 foot pas-"sengers and 90 vehicles in half-an-hour, how "many would be obstructed at Windmill point "where there is but one thoroughfare."

Again:—

"In this comparison we are giving Mr. Young the advantage of his concealing us he does the possibility of the said foot passengers and vehicles finding their way over some of the other 'fourteen great thoroughfares.'"

If Mr. Workman will examine Mr. Trautwine's plan, he will find that ten of the "fourteen thoroughfares" are stopped up by the Docks and not provided with bridges; that there are only four drawbridges;—that the distance between each of these fourteen thoroughfares is only 180 feet, and that drawbidges could not be erected for these "fourteen thoroughfares" for the reason that 180 feet would not allow sufficient space for a vessel to lie, and instead of there being only one bridge across the Canal at Windmill Point, there is another at Wellington Bridge, and there should also be two more constructed at the foot of McGill Street, and on the same level, across the Canal there, to communicate with the Docks, by filling up the water space around Windmill Point. It is a mistake, however, to suppose that the Docks would increase cartage across the Canal. Property, whether merchandise or produce, intended for city use, would then be landed as now on the city side of the Canal and in the Harbour. The Docks would serve, and are intended to serve a purpose similar to that of the Atlantic Docks at New York, for receiving and delivering produce, provisions, merchandise, &c., intendeded for export, by sea, or inland to the Eastern or Western States. Mr. Workman next takes exception to my statement, that if Mr. Trautwine's Dock scheme was carried out, the water would have to be "drawn off the Canal in winter, and for such withdrawal of wate every factory on the Canal would have a claim for damages." Equally unfortunate with the "fourteen thoroughfares." Look at the lease again, Mr Workman, and you will find that the withdrawal of water "for repairs, improvements or alterations" refers to Canal improvements, and that the lessees have no right to demand damage for any withdrawal of water for such repairs or improvements of the Canal; but the withdrawal of water to construct a Dock, is not a withdrawal of water for Canal repairs or improvements, and that therefore my statement that the lessees would have a claim for damages is correct in every particular. Again, if Mr. Workman will look he will find that I am also correct in stating that the water level of Mr. Trautwine's scheme of Docks "is five feet higher than McGill Street, "or any of the streets in Griffintown, and that "the Dock wharves will be five feet higher than "the water, hence no point of the wharves could "be reached from Wellington or McGill Street, except by an ascent of 10 feet."

An amusing instance of Mr. Workman's acuteness will be found in his reference to the value of the land required for docks according to the various schemes. He says:—"I next come to Mr. Young's objection to the valuations of the land required for Mr. Trautwine's scheme of docks. In page 47 Mr. Young says:—'But again, according to Mr. Trautwine's scheme, I find that a gross error has been committed in estimating the value of the land proposed to be taken for the dock project.'"

The error referred to was simply this: Mr. Trautwine's scheme was compared with the Point St. Charles scheme, as to its cost; one element in the cost is the extent and value of the land. Mr. Trautwine's docks required an area of 120 acres, and the estimate of the value of the land only covered eighteen acres. The land at Point St. Charles formed part of the harbor, and would not require to be paid for. The land for Mr. Trautwine's scheme to a great extent, say nearly 91 acres was on the south side of the canal. This was clearly stated in my letter, and the cost of the 91 acres put down at $309,400 as an item to be added to the cost of Mr. Trautwine's scheme of docks. The error consisted in omitting this item, on the ground that the land belonged to the Government or the Grand Trunk, and therefore *need not be paid for*

Mr. Workman appears to misunderstand what the error was. He produces letters from Messrs. Spiers & Son, which shew that the land at their valuation was put at 2s 3d per foot, and in Messrs Brown and Watson's at 2s 2½d, making in land and buildings on the *north side* of the canal a difference of $65,805 between the estimates, and adds that, from Messrs. Spier & Son's note, " it appears that the gross error which he charges Mr. Trautwine with is his own, as it arises simply from Mr. Young's valuators, Messrs. Brown and Watson having taken more land for Mr. Trautwine's project than Mr. Trautwine himself asked " " Here, then, is the extent of the gross error committed, $65,805." If Mr. Workman had shewn, either that the cost of the 91 acres should not have been added to Mr. Trautwine's estimate, because the land belonged to Government or to the Grand Trunk, he would have met the argument. But this would have been a difficult task, and it was easier to avoid the real point, and demolish a supposed argument, and then coolly fix the "gross error" upon me, giving the " Canadian I " a slap, and at the same time patronizing and patting on the head, Messrs. Spiers & Son, by adding, " those acquainted with Messrs. Spiers & Son's high character for such judgment and correct business talent will have little apprehension as to where the error lies."

There are many other points in Mr. Workman's letters in relation to docks and the trade of the Port, on which I might touch, but the subject has become wearisome, and I shall proceed to notice a charge which I deem of graver importance. In my letter of 10th December I stated, in reference to the dock and other projects having been stamped as "visionary," and as "vague dreams of the imagination" by Mr. Trautwine, that " it should be remembered that other projects advocated by me, which at first were considered as unfavorably as the dock at Point St. Charles, have been carried out. I allude to the deepening of Lake St. Peter in the old channel, which was recommended by me in a Report to the Board of Trade in 1846, and which was at first covered with ridicule, but which was

lina. adopted and the works commenced by Government, and abandoned after an expenditure of £75,000." These remarks were fully justified by the facts of the case. In supreme ignorance of these facts, and with his usual recklessness, Mr Workman seizes upon the statement as an assumption on my part of merit, which he thinks does not belong to me. On the contrary he believes that my conduct in reference to the Lake St. Peter operations is deserving of censure, and that but for me, a far different and more advantageous state of things, for the trade of the city and country, would now have been secured. This is rather an important statement, coming as it does from Mr. Workman, who styles himself " A Merchant," and who ought to be intimately acquainted with all the facts, and therefore I trust I shall be excused from giving a brief outline of the circumstances which led the Harbour Commissioners to be connected with the deepening of Lake St Peter. I do this the more readily, because it cannot be a matter devoid of interest to your readers and to the public, to be reminded of the facts concerning a work which lies at the very foundation of our city's progress and advancement in trade, facts which Mr. Workman should have ascertained before he made the assertion contained in his letter.

But I must defer the further consideration of this matter till my next letter, and am, now,

Your obedient servant,

JOHN YOUNG.

Montreal, July 26th, 1859.

To the Editor of THE MONTREAL GAZETTE:

SIR,—I closed my last letter by stating that, in supreme ignorance of the facts in reference to the deepening of Lake St. Peter and the improvement of the navigation in other parts of the river between Quebec and Montreal, Mr Workman considered my remarks in my letter of 10th December, as an assumption of merit on my part, and that instead of deserving any commendation for my exertions for so improving the navigation, as to enable steamers and vessels of large size to ascend the river to our Harbour, I in fact deserved censure.

That the public may judge of this charge, I give the following extracts from Mr. Workman's letters. These I quote at some length, as I do not wish to imitate his example by partial extracts quoted as applicable to other points than those to which they were intended to apply :—

"It is to be hoped that the citizens will be awake on this point Let them remember that at present they suffer heavily in harbour taxation from the unjust burthen of the deepening of Lake St Peter, which, instead of being a Provincial work, just as clearly as any canal, lock or lighthouse from Burlington Bay to Belleisle Straits, has been thrown, by the action of Mr. Young, since the year 1845, on the trade of the city of Montreal solely.

About the period mentioned, the Government had made considerable progress in making a straight channel, *at the public cost*, through Lake St. Peter. A strong opposition to this channel, arising apparently out of local and personal jealousies as to the appointment of a Superintendent, was got up by Mr. Young and others. The works had been in operation nearly two years, and had progressed till within 352,000 yards of completion. For a channel 150 feet wide and 14 feet deep it required only about 152 days additional work to complete the channel, but the opposition was so annoying to a weak Government, who were not reluctant to avail themselves of any excuse to stop the expenditure, that the works were suspended. A Commission was then appointed to enquire into the subject and report as to best channel. This Commission was composed of Messrs. John Redpath, Hon. F. A. Quesnel and M. J. Hays, and after minute inspection, personal examination and taking evidence on both sides, they made an elaborate Report approving of the action of the Board of Works in selecting the straight channel, as may be seen from the following extract from their Report :—

"The Commissioners, after mature considera-
"tion of the information derived from the various
"sources, have come to the following conclu-
"sion :

"That the new and straight line adopted by
"the Board of Works and now in progress, is
"preferable to the old and circuitous channel;
"and that the Chairman of the Board is fully
"borne out in the adoption of this line by the
"valuable testimony of Captain Bayfield and
"other scientific men in England."

Notwithstanding this decided Report of the Commissioners in favor of the straight channel, Mr. Young and his party kept up th opposition to it, and, rather than it should be completed, they consented to an act *placing the entire cost of the deepening of Lake St. Peter upon the trade of our Port instead of continuing it as a Provincial work at the public cost, as it had been by the previous Act which Mr. Young destroyed*. The entire expenditure in constructing the straight channel so near to its completion, thus became a dead loss to the country, and the future cost of the work was thrown upon the City of Montreal Who, upon perusing these facts and turning to Mr. Young's self-laudation on the "deepening of Lake St. Peter" and the frequent allusion he makes to it, in connection with the benefits (?) he has bestowed on Montreal, can repress a

smile? In the pamphlet before us Mr. Young says :—

"Entertaining these views, it is not to be won-
"dered at if I have persisted in keeping them be-
"fore the public, although they should be stamped
"as visionary, and as vague dreams of the imagi-
"nation. It should also be remembered that
"other projects advocated by me, which at first
"were considered as unfavorable as the Dock
"at Point St. Charles, have been carried out.

"I allude to the deepening of Lake St. Peter
"in the old channel, which was recommended
"by me in 1846, and was at first covered with
"ridicule, but which was finally adopted, and
"the Government works abandoned after an
"expenditure of about £75,000."

"Seventy-five thousand" pounds! Don Quixote again! The *entire* expenditure, as may be seen by the Report of the Commissioners, was £59,-994 1s. 0d.,—but of this there were £37,937 9s. 5½ expended upon steamers and dredging boats, scows and outfit which apparatus being available for the works on the crooked channel, leaves the actual expenditure for deepening the straight channel only £22,056 11s. 7d.

"Covered with ridicule"—what ridicule? The entire discussion was confined to the question of *filling up* by drifting sand banks, and the *time* it would require to make the straight channel.

The Commissioners report "That they had
"scarcely entered upon their duties when their
"attention was directed to the works in ques-
"tion, by persons *proffering their testimony* to
"prove that the straight line adopted by the
"Board of Works for the new channel would
"never answer the purpose intended, that it
"would require fifteen or twenty years for its
"completion, at a great outlay of money, and
"that it would fill up nearly as fast as it was
'made."

The impartiality of this evidence may be appreciated, by allusion to the two points it aims at. The *filling up* and the *time* needed to complete the straight line.

The Commissioners shew, as before observed, that an excavation of 352,000 yards, requiring 152 days time, would complete the channel ; and, if the Government had been allowed to proceed, we would have had the channel in 1846, instead of 15 or 20 years later, and for a comparatively small outlay over and above what then had been expended ; and, to use the words of the Commissioners, "the trade would thus be in possession
"of two channels, of which one might be made to
"serve for vessels for whose draft of water it
"might be suitable—the other to serve for ves-
"sels of a larger draft. The risk of collision
"would thus be very much reduced." As to the questions of filling up, the Commissioners took great pains to obtain reliable information on that point, by causing soundings to be taken in the fall and spring, with a view of ascertaining if the spring floods had any effect upon the new cut. The result was, that "they found that no
"perceptible filling up had taken place, but that
"the cut remained in the same state as when the
"dredges left it"

There is no question but the straight channel would have answered every purpose, and could have been easily deepened or widened as circumstances would require. The Town of Belfast, some years ago, attempted to improve, at an immense cost, the crooked natural channel leading into their port, but it was found difficult to keep it open, and a straight new channel was finally cut, which suits much better. When the merchants, ship-owners and steamboat proprietors of Montreal, and the poor *habitans* who cross with their loaded vehicles on these ferry-boats, consider the exorbitant wharfage they are compelled to pay, a large portion of which goes to meet the cost of Mr. Young's Lake St. Peter folly, and to enable Upper Canada merchants to bring their goods by ocean craft 180 miles nearer their own door, at our expense, in place of at the public cost, as it would have been, had Mr. Young stood back, they can appreciate the boon conveyed by " the "deepening of Lake St. Peter in the old channel, "which was recommended by me (Mr. Young) "in 1846."

So much for Mr. Workman's views as to the "deepening of Lake St. Peter." Now for the facts.

From 1832 to 1840, the merchants and citizens of Montreal at various times brought before the attention of the Government, by petitions, the great injury which resulted to the trade of the Province from the shallowness of Lake St. Peter, and the imperative necessity which existed for deepening it. These representations induced the Government of the Province, in 1836, to refer the whole subject to a Committee of the House of Assembly, which Committee reported, in favour of the work being undertaken as a Provincial work. Capt. Bay field, R.N., was called before this Committee, and was asked:—"From your knowledge of " that part of the St Lawrence (Lake St. Peter), " do you think it would be practicable to deepen " the channel, so as to allow vessels of a greater " burthen to proceed to Montreal than its depth " at present admits?" Capt. Bayfield said that —"It may be done by excavating the present " channel through the St. Francis shoal for a " distance of two miles, by which, however, only " six inches, or at most one foot, increase of " depth would be gained. To obtain a greater " depth, a channel must be excavated through " the flats of Lake St. Peter four and a half nau- " tical miles in length, a work which would re- " quire so much time and labour that, with the " means contemplated, it is not impossible that " the end first excavated, might be filled up by " sand washing in, by the time the other was " reached. The magnitude of such a work will " be best understood by the statement that, if it " were contemplated only to obtain an addi- " tional increase of two feet in depth, and to

" limit the excavation to 200 feet—and it could " not well be less, to allow vessels to turn in " and to pass each other without risk—no less " than eleven million of cubic feet of soil would " have to be removed to effect it." Nothing, however, was done till 1840, when authority was obtained from Parliament to begin the work. In 1841 and 1842, Chas. Atherton, Esq., who had then great experience in the Clyde works, and is now a distinguished Civil Engineer in H.M.S. at Woolwich, was employed by the Board of Works in Canada to survey and report upon the best means of deepening Lake St. Peter. This he did, in a Report dated August 1843. This document is too long for insertion in these letters, I shall, therefore, quote only the principal points of it. Mr. Atherton says—

" The Board is in possession of other surveys, but it is necessary to fix upon some one survey as the Map of Reference, and it is my duty to recommend that Bayfield's be taken for that purpose, which I think *admirably correct*. On the general subject my previous correspondence has already apprised the Board *that*, in my opinion, *the only means of attaining the object in view —a passage for deep-draft vessels—is by selecting the existing channel as the line of operations*, limiting our works to the dredging out a narrow cut —I may call it a sunk canal—whereby the improved channel may be indicated day and night. But, on the present occasion of final decision, the Board may be desirous of having before them the various views which have been promulgated, and I may briefly adduce the reasons which have led me to recommend a strict adherence to the improvement of the old channel, in preference to adopting other plans which have been brought before the public notice :

1st. It has been proposed to form a straight channel through the Lake, taking advantage of the stretch of a pool of 13 feet of water which extends from off the mouth of the River St. Francis into deep water at Pointe du Lac. I cannot concur in this project because it involves the necessity of cutting through the *main body*, (not clipping off the extremity) of the St. Francis bank, which bank extends out into the middle of the Lake opposite Riviere du Loup. The width of the bank to be cut through would be about two and a half miles, and after all the channel thus proposed to be attained by cutting through the St. Francis bank gives only 12 to 13 feet water, and would therefore require dredging over a further extent of about 8½ miles before it meets the 14 feet water opposite Machiche.

2nd. It has been also proposed to close several of the minor channels between the islands at the head of the Lake. I cannot concur in this view, for although it be granted that the main body of the St. Lawrence might be confined to one of the main channels, still the scouring effect thus produced would be lost as soon as the water would have liberty to spread, and a shoal would undoubtedly be formed where the scouring effect ceases

3rd. Another plan has been the construction of a Dam across the outlet of the Lake near Pointe du Lac, whereby the surface of the Lake may be raised to such height as may be necessary for the purpose of the navigation. Even admitting all this were effected, the Lake would be converted into a sort of cesspool, having a gradual tendency to equalisation throughout."

In October, 1843, the Secretary of the Board of Works wrote to Mr. Atherton "that the Board " propose, during the interval between the pre- " sent and opening of the working season next " spring, to collect from all quarters, where " knowledge of the Lake and other requisites " may appear to them to exist, the fullest advice " and information, by the general result of which " they will be guided in their decision as to the " channel to be adopted." In January, 1844, the Board of Works dispatched Capt. Vaughan, with a letter from Mr. Killaly, to Captain Bayfield, then in Prince Edwards Island, but without sending to that officer the Reports of Mr. Atherton.

Mr. Killaly asks for Captain Bayfield's opinion, stating that his "idea would be first to " obtain a direct channel of moderate breadth " and 12 feet deep throughout, and subsequently " to be governed in adding to its depth and " breadth by circumstances. The facility that " exists for directing a column of water from two " or three of the present channels into the new " one, is, I think, much in favor of adopting the " straight channel." In the representations made to Capt. Bayfield, through Captain Vaughan and others, it will afterwards be seen that this able officer felt himself deceived, in giving the following opinion under date of 12th February, 1858 :

" My opinion has never been decidedly adverse to the attempt to deepen Lake St Peter, as you have been informed ; but I have always viewed it, *and still do view it as a work of too great magnitude, importance and difficulty* to be lightly undertaken, or proceeded on without all that cautious regard to the effect of the work as it proceeds. I quite agree with you that the old channel, shewn by the blue line on the trace, should be abandoned, and the attempt made in the direction indicated by the red line, because it would require only about two nautical miles of excavation to give a depth of 12 to 13 feet at low water, if the depth has not diminished since our last survey, and if even the advantage gained should be limited to the attainment of a depth of 12 or 13 feet, in a direct instead of a circuitous channel, the benefit to the navigation would, I conceive, be very great. *But it would require no less than five miles cutting by the old route, and nine miles by the proposed new and direct channel, to obtain a depth of 14 feet, which I conjess appears to me a herculean task.*"

This important work of deepening Lake St. Peter was therefore begun in the Spring of 1844, with the view of making a straight channel of 150 feet wide and 14 feet deep at low water, against the very strong opinions of Mr. Atherton, who had spent two seasons in the examination of the whole matter, and whose opinions never were submitted to Captain Bayfield. The work attracted the attention of the late Admiral Boxer, then Captain of the Port of Quebec, also of Colonel Halloway, who were engaged in the survey of the St. Lawrence by the direction of the Home Government. These gent'emen were assisted by Lieut. Moody. R. E., and Mr. Taylor, and found so great a difference between the actual soundings in Lake St. Peter, by the proposed channels, and those furnished by the Board of Works, that they felt compelled to address the Governor General on the subject (June 1845). They say,—

" That on our survey down the river, from Montreal to the Pillars, we examined Lake St. Peter, and we were very particular in doing so, as we had good reason to believe that Mr Killaly had been deceived by the Reports which had been made to him, and which was proved, by sounding, where we only found 12 feet where 17 was laid down, and only six inches between the two channels, whereas the survey we had received from the Board of Works *shewed a difference of two feet.*"

Mr. Atherton finding his views could not be carried out, left the employ of the Government and went to England in 1844. From the commencement of the work, and up to 1846, the deepening of Lake St. Peter was much discussed, and was disapproved of by the Pilots, and by Charles Armstrong, Esq., present Superintendent of Lake Improvements. and J. D. Armstrong, Esq., Harbour Master of Quebec. These gentlemen were then commanders of the Tug Steamers on the St. Lawrence, and really had a more practical knowledge of the subject than almost any other parties. In 1846 I was elected as one of the Council of the Board of Trade. Up to that time I had taken no part in the discussion as to the channel which should be deepened, but I was then strongly impressed *that the future of Montreal, as a great seat of commerce, depended on the capacity of the channel being able to allow vessels of the largest tonnage to ascend to Montreal without breaking bulk.* Under this impression I took an early opportunity of directing the attention of my colleagues to the great importance of the subject, which resulted in a Resolution being unanimously passed, requesting me to accompany Messrs. Quesnel, Redpath and Hayes to Lake St. Peter. These gentlemen had been named by Government as Commissioners to examine into the disputed advantages of the straight channel. Up to this time I had not taken any part in the dispute, nor indeed did I understand it. Messrs. Redpath and Hayes alone went to Lake St. Peter, and were not accompanied by Mr. Quesnel, as stated by Mr. Workman. The late Admiral Boxer, Capt. C. L. Armstrong, and two Branch Pilots, Messrs. Coté and Hamelin, were also there,—and I was present while the soundings were taken in both channels. Messrs. Redpath and Hayes reported, as Mr. Workman states, in favor of the straight channel. The calculation of the amount of soil to be removed from either channel, was a very simple one, and in this respect I did not differ with Messrs. Redpath and Hayes; but I held *that even then* the old channel was the best, in every respect, and that it would cost much less money to deepen it, and, moreover, that it was clear to my mind that a great blunder had been committed by not having chosen the old channel for improvement, and that the attempt to deepen the straight channel should be at once abandoned. It was to this effect I reported to the Council of the Board of Trade in 1846. I must, however, defer further consideration of this subject till my next letter, and am,

Your obedient servant,

JOHN YOUNG.

Montreal, 27th July, 1859.

LETTER NO 9.

To the Editor of the MONTREAL GAZETTE:

SIR,—In concluding my last letter, in reference to Lake St. Peter improvements, I stated that while Messrs. Redpath and Hayes reported to the Government that " the new and straight " line adopted by the Board of Works, and now " in process, is preferable to the old and circuit- " ous channel, and that the Chairman of the " Board is fully borne out in the adoption of " this line by the valuable testimony of Captain " Bayfield, and other scientific men in England." I believed that I saw enough to satisfy me, that the operations of the Board of Works, were a great blunder, and that the dredging should have been carried on in the old or natural chan-

nel. Under this impression I made my Report to the Council of the Board of Trade in 1846, and after reporting to the Board the quantity of material to be removed to give a depth of 14 feet at low water, I stated that " in my opin- "ion, after very careful enquiry from experienced " men, the proposed breadth of 150 feet *is not* " *sufficient* to render the navigation safe, and " that it would require a much greater breadth. "The only objection to the natural channel is " the fact of its not being straight, but this has " not heretofore been found of any consequence. " The great breadth and necessary depth of " water for a large part of the distance in the "old channel, and parallel to the new channel " now being deepened, are to my mind to be "preferred to any advantages which the new " channel offers, and I have no hesitation in re- "commending that future labour should be " expended in deepening the natural channel— "*and that the new channel should be abandoned.*"

This report was not adopted by the Council of the Board of Trade,—indeed, it was rather laughed at. Shortly after this in the same year, a select Committee was named by the House of Assembly to examine and report on this vexed question of the Lake St. Peter improvement. The Committee was composed of several naval and scientific men, and although I was not present with them or knew them personally, they did me the honour of alluding to my Report to the Board of Trade, and after some complimentary re- marks, say that " Mr. Young then estimates " that the excavation required in the natural " channel to make it navigable the entire length " for vessels drawing 14 feet of water, and 150 feet " wide, would be 352,000 cubic yards, making it " only one-sixteenth part less than your Com- " mittee."

The Committee unanimously recommended that the works in the new channel should be abandoned, and say " that your Committee have "failed to discover any rational motives for the " adoption of the new cut in preference to the " improvement of the old channel, and can only " imagine that such decision may have been made, " and the work proceeded with, without any esti- "mate of the relative expense of the respective " channels." After this Report was presented to the House of Assembly, the Government, in the same year (1846), by an order in Council, made application to the Imperial government, request- ing that Capt. Bayfield be sent from England to Canada, to examine and report on the disputed channels, and to make such further observations as would tend to guide the government in the course which should be pursued. Captain Bayfield came to Canada, and in September, 1846, reported at great length on the whole subject. That able officer was obliged to confess that, after three seasons' work in the new channel: *the expense of deepening the old channel to 14 feet at low water* would be £15,300 11s 3d *less* than to deepen the straight channel, even improved as it then was. Captain Bayfield, in alluding to the advantages and disadvantages of the two channels, says :—

" Before I attempt, in conclusion, the somewhat difficult task of balancing these conflicting advantages and disadvantages, I beg to observe that the question is no longer the same as before the commencement of the work, since a large sum has been expended. *If, in the first instance, when I was consulted before the commencement of the works, it had been represented to me that the amount of excavation required to deepen the new channel, and consequently the expense would be nearly double that required in the old channel, instead of its having been inconsiderately stated to me by an authority, the competency of which I could not doubt, that on a comparison of the two channels it was found that the quantity to remove from the straight channel was ' but little more than what would be necessary in the crooked one,' I would have doubted whether any advantages possessed by the new channel could have afforded a sufficient compensation for so great a difference of expense, and been compelled to decide in favour of the line of the old channel.*"   *   *   *   *

Let Mr. Workman bear in mind that this report of Captain Bayfield's bears out the correctness in every particular, of my statement to the Board of Trade. Captain Bayfield however, in conse quence of the money already expended and under the belief that a 14 foot channel only was required, advised the Government to proceed with the straight channel. Up to this time there was no proposal to make a channel deeper than 14 feet.

Again Captain Bayfield says:—

* * * " We have in the old channel the sole but important advantage of its width down as far as the lower light house : an advantage so great, that if the intention were to *make a channel for all purposes, it could only be compensated by cutting through the bank of St. Francis, a channel at least 600 feet wider* than has been intended (or 900 feet in all) "

The Report of Captain Bayfield was referred to a Select Committee of the House of Assembly, in July, 1847, who reported that—" The Com- " mittee have in evidence, that the cut through " the St. Francis Bank to make the artificial " channel through Lake St. Peter, was under- " taken on erroneous data of the contemplated " expenditure, and seriously at variance with

" what might have reasonably been anticipated." " That the sum of £400,000 would be insufficient " to secure its ultimate completion, if completed " to the breadth of 900 feet and 14 feet deep, as " recommended by Captain Bayfield, and that " portion of the old natural channel which has " a breadth of 1500 feet, and a depth of 18 to 20 " feet for a distance of 4½ miles down to the " lower light-house, would at all times be more " advantageous to vessels of all classes, both by " night and day ; and the Committee recommend " that nothing more should be expended beyond " the amount of the appropriation of last ses- " sion."

The work was thus abandoned by the Government, as, indeed, all the other public works were, at the same time stopped by the want of funds to proceed with them. Mr. Workman, no doubt recollects the issue by the Government of the notes which were then called " shin-plasters," and that it was impossible at that time to proceed with any public work. So, that, even supposing that my Report in favour of the abandonment of the work had been disregarded, the works in Lake St. Peter would have been stopped nevertheless, as all other roads and works were then stopped, from want of funds to carry them on.

Beyond my examination in 1846, and my Report advising that the work should be discontinued, I had nothing to do with the matter until the Spring of 1850, when I was appointed a Harbour Commissioner. In 1847, 1848, and 1849, the Board of Trade on various occasions brought the subject of the improvement of Lake St. Peter before the Government, and urged with vigour its great importance to the trade of the country, and pointed out the vast expense of lighterage between Quebec and Montreal.

In the Public Works Report of 1848, signed by the Hon. Malcolm Cameron and Sir E. P. Taché, these gentlemen state " that they had " examined the two channels, and that but " few persons now refuse to acknowledge that if " the money which has been employed in exca- " vating the new channel (still incomplete) had " been expended in improving the old and natu- " ral channel, the commerce of the country " would have been in possession of a navigation " through Lake St. Peter, equal at all seasons " of the year to the depth which can be obtained " at other points of the river."

In April, 1850, I brought the subject of deepening Lake St. Peter before my colleagues in the Harbour Commission, (Messrs. John Try and Louis Marchand,) and my plans for carrying out the work were submitted to the Provincial Secretary, the Hon Jas. Leslie. The mode of doing so was entirely different from anything which had been previously suggested, and may be stated as follows :—

That the Harbour Commissioners of Montreal should be authorised to undertake the work and to borrow a certain sum of money for the purpose, the interests or the sums borrowed as well as a sinking fund of two per cent. per annum to be provided for as follows : First, by a tonnage duty of not exceeding one shilling per Register ton, on all vessels drawing ten feet of water and upwards, such duty to be levied for each time of passing the Lake ; secondly, by the surplus revenues of the Harbour of Montreal in case such tonnage duty should prove insufficient for the purpose ; and thirdly, that the Governor General should have authority to empower the Harbour Commissioners to levy such additional per centage on all their Harbour and Lake dues as would in his opinion afford them a sufficient revenue to meet every legal charge upon it. This plan was adopted by the Government, and an Act of Parliament procured in accordance with it. The first step taken was, at my suggestion, to appoint a Board of Engineers to examine Lake St. Peter and report upon the best course to be pursued for the purpose of obtaining therein, a ship channel of 16 feet in depth at low water, being two feet deeper than the channel contemplated by the Commissioners of Public Works or by any other parties. The gentlemen selected for this important duty, were Messrs. McNeil and Child, eminent Civil Engineers of the United States, and Mr. Gzowski, a well known Civil Engineer of Canada, and these gentlemen, accompanied by Sir W. S. Logan, Provincial Geologist, who kindly lent his services to determine the nature and the origin of the materials constituting the obstacles to be removed, made a minute survey of the old and new channels, and after mature deliberation thereon, recommended the Harbour Commissioners not to resume operations in the straight cut attempted by the Commissioners of the Public Works, but on the contrary, to follow the channel already formed by natural causes, which they reported, presented no obstructions but sand and clay which could easily be removed by dredging. That course was adopted by the Harbour Commissioners, and the most complete success has been the result.

It may be well here to refer to a charge of inaccuracy made against me, with his usual success, of giving it to be understood that the works in Lake St. Peter, abandoned by the Government, cost the country £75,000. Mr. Workman states that after deducting dredges and scows handed over to the Harbour Commissioners, that the actual loss was only £22,056 11s. 7d. If Mr. Workman will examine the public accounts, he will find that "Lake St. Peter" stands debited with £73,553 15s. 5d. *without any interest.* The two dredges handed over to the Harbour Commissioners, had been in use four seasons and were eight years old, and took so much to put them in repair, that the engines only were worth anything. The same may be said of the two old scows—so that my remark is strictly correct. The progress of the work may be again brought before the public in the following statement :—

The Harbour Commissioners commenced operations on the 12th June, 1851, with one dredge and the Harrow, and on the 3rd of November in the same year a channel 75 feet wide, two feet deep, and four miles in length was cut through the highest part of the flats. On the 8th of November the ship 'City of Manchester' was loaded down to fourteen feet, the depth on the flats then being twelve feet, and taken through the Lake without slackening speed. Thus in less than five months two feet were added to the draught of sea-going vessels trading with Montreal. In the Spring of 1852 the Harrow was employed during high water, in May and June, upon the upper bar, the depth upon which was thereby increased about three feet, leaving a channel one hundred and fifty feet wide and fifteen feet deep, at low water, or four feet deeper than the flats. Two dredges worked on the flats from the latter part of May until the 16th of Nov., by which time they had widened the channel (from seventy-five) to one hundred and fifty feet, and deepened it (from two) to four feet. The length of the channel of 1851 was also increased (from four miles) to five and a half miles,—this additional length of dredging being required in consequence of the increased depth. Thus at the close of the second season, or in less than eleven months of actual work, a channel one hundred and fifty feet in width, and four feet of additional depth was cut through the ' flats' and the upper bar at a cost of £47,250 for operations and outfit, or in other words, a channel of the same width and one foot greater depth, than that which the Government *had failed to secure* in the new route with a far greater expenditure of time and money. The Harbour Commissioners were notified in November, 1852, by the Superintendent that he was then prepared to take a vessel through the Lake drawing four feet more water than any which had hitherto left Montreal at that season of the year. Throughout the season of '52 the sea-going vessels made use of the new channel and many of them were loaded down two feet deeper than the water on the flats.

A vessel of sufficient capacity could not be obtained at that late season of the year, to test the capacity of the channel, in November, 1852, but this was done on the 24th of August, 1853, by the barque 'California,' which was loaded down to sixteen feet two inches, when there was only twelve feet on the flats and taken from Montreal through the Lake, without delay or difficulty.

At the close of the season of 1853 the channel of 1853 was deepened throughout, one foot six inches, giving sixteen and a half feet at low water, and a part of it was widened (from one hundred and fifty feet) to two hundred and fifty and three hundred feet."

Having anticipated the remarkable success already stated, the Harbour Commissioners, in 1853, thought it desirable to ascertain whether any and what obstacles existed in the River St. Lawrence to deepening the channel to 20 feet at low water, being satisfied that carrying their operations in Lake St. Peter to that depth was merely a question of time and money that could easily be determined. They accordingly directed their Engineer, Mr. T. C. Keefer, to make such a survey of the River and Lake between Montreal and Quebec as would enable him to report what impediments did exist thereto, and what the probable cost of removing them would be. By the end of October, 1853, Mr. Keefer (assisted by Captain Bell, under whose superintendence the operations had hitherto been conducted) had made such progress that he was able to report the entire practicability of deepening the channel to 20 feet at low water between Montreal and Quebec, provided that a channel on the south shore of the River St Lawrence between Varennes and Lavaltrie (to which Captain Bell had previously drawn the attention of the Harbour Commissioners) was adopted for improvement instead of the old channel hitherto used by pilots on the north side of the river. The Harbour Commissioners resolved that it was expedient to adopt the course

recommended by Mr. Keefer, and to carry on the deepening to 20 feet at low water, provided the Board of Trade of Montreal approved of their doing so. A resolution to this effect was accordingly submitted to the Board of Trade, which was unanimously approved of. The citizens also, at a public meeting specially called to consider the subject, sanctioned it without a dissenting voice.

Mr. Keefer says " that although the straight " channel would have shortened the route " through the lake, yet, as it was wholly an ar- " tificial one, there was a greater amount of work " to be done in it. Captain Bayfield *in* 1846, " (after 3 years dredging in the straight channel,) " estimated the dredging *then to be done* in the " straight channel for a depth of only 14 feet at " low water, at 260,000 cubic yards more than " that required to produce the same result in the " old channel. In extending the work, however, " to a depth of 20 feet, the economy of the old " channel is much more apparent. In order to give " three hundred feet in width, with 20 feet of " water in the 'straight' channel *would now re-* " *quire no less than one million eight hundred* " *and ten thousand and eight cubic yards to be* " *be removed more than is requisite to produce* " *the same result in the old channel.*" This, too, let it be borne in mind, that when so deepened, the old channel for nearly half the distance would be 1500 feet wide, while the straight channel for the same distance would have been only 300 feet wide.

My fellow-citizens, and the public generally, can now judge how far I am justified in taking to myself credit for these great results. It is true that my Report in 1846, recommending that future labour should be done in the old, and not in the new channel, contributed largely to the abandonment of the work in the latter; but, with the facts, and opinions of professional men of the highest standing, and by others, will any one pretend to say that but for the stopping of the new cut we could have had to-day a channel 18 feet deep at the lowest water, and 300 feet wide, with the prospect of a 20 foot channel in two years. I have shewn that the valuable opinion of Mr. Atherton, in favour of deepening the natural channel, after a careful and elaborate survey of two seasons, was disregarded--an opinion too, which was supported by every scientific man who afterwards examined the subject—and that this all-important work was proceeded with in the straight channel, by the Department of Public

Works, against the advice and report of its own officer. It is true that Captain Bayfield's name was drawn in to support the conclusions of the Department of Public Works, but I have shewn that this opinion was obtained from Capt Bayfield by unfounded representations from, as that officer states, "an authority the competency " of which I could not doubt." The results confirm in every respect, the correctness of the valuable opinions of Mr. Atherton and of Messrs. Childe, Gzowski, McNiel, and Keefer, which is very creditable to those gentlemen ; but at the same time the bungling and blundering of the Department of Public Works is equally apparent, and I may well ask whether my conduct in 1846, in exposing this blunder, deserves praise or censure ?

But I must defer my further remarks, on what Mr. Workman is pleased to designate "Mr. Young's Lake St. Peter folly," till my next letter, and am now,

Your obedient servant,
JOHN YOUNG.

Montreal, 2nd August, 1859.

LETTER NO. 10.

To the Editor of the MONTREAL GAZETTE :

SIR,—It has not, I believe, been questioned that the general public interest would be promoted by such an improvement of the navigation, between Quebec and Montreal, as would enable the largest class of vessels to ascend the latter port from sea without breaking bulk. I have shewn that as early as 1830, the merchants and citizens of Montreal were unanimous in pointing out to the Government the enormous annual loss to the trade of the Province, which resulted from the necessity of lighterage over the shallows of Lake St. Peter,—and the unanimity which prevailed, in urging upon the Government, the necessity of removing as speedily as possible so great a drawback to the interior and city trade. I have shewn also, that Government and Parliament in 1840 acknowledged the correctness of these representations, by the adoption of measures to deepen the channel through Lake St. Peter—that Mr. Atherton's advice was discarded and a plan adopted by the Department of Public Works, and Captain Bayfield's sanction thereto was obtained by false representations made to that officer—that after three seasons' work, and an expenditure of £75,000, it was shewn by my Report to the Board of Trade in 1846, that a great blunder had been committed

by selecting a new and straight channel through the Lake, instead of deepening the old or natural channel, and that it was in every way preferable to abandon what had been done and begin anew. This opinion, as has been stated, was confirmed by the Committee of the House of Assembly, and by all the scientific men, who afterwards examined the subject. The work was, therefore, abandoned. Moreover, it has been shewn, that had the work not been so abandoned, it would have been almost impossible, from the great cost, to have obtained the proposed channel of twenty feet at low water.

Before I took the matter in hand, as Harbour Commissioner, *no one* had suggested a greater depth than 14 feet. Captain Bayfield, it will be seen, in 1836, looked upon the work as almost impossible, because of the magnitude of deepening it only two feet, and of removing 11,000,000 cubic feet. Yet, to-day, upwards of fifty millions of cubic feet of soil have been removed, and the channel deepened seven feet. To enable your readers to form an opinion of the amount of labour necessary to produce such a great result, I may state that Captain Bayfield, in a Report dated 1844, says " that to deepen the channel " to 14 feet only, and 300 feet wide, for a " distance of nine miles, seemed to him a " hercu- " lean task." Yet it would seem that after this "herculean" work was accomplished, a work is progressing to successful completion, five times greater than that deemed "herculean" by Captain Bayfield. Again, a channel of 14 feet would not have allowed the large sized sailing vessels to come to Montreal without breaking bulk, neither could the magnificent steamers, which now arrive in port, have come here. I have it in my power to shew that the present depth of water and the proposed depth is not only beneficial in the highest degree to Montreal as a port, but lies at the very foundation of the future greatness of the city. It is also equally beneficial to the country, inasmuch as it lessens the distance from the interior to a sea port 180 miles, and by cheapening transport enhances the value of every agricultural commodity exported. I have labored for several years, and have succeeded in obtaining the acknowledgment of this and former governments that the works in Lake St. Peter and the St. Lawrence are not local in their character, but should be considered as Provincial Public Works. Already, indeed, the Government have so far acknowledged this, that a sum of £15,000 has been advanced by Government for the Lake St. Peter operations of this year.

But Mr. Workman, a wealthy and leading citizen, sees no merit in my having been the means of putting a stop to the progress of the blunder of the Board of Works in Lake St. Peter, nor in my labours during the last ten years, to make Montreal a port accessible for vessels and steamers of 2,400 tons burthen. The slightest investigation of the subject will satisfy any one, that had not the straight channel been discontinued, it would have been impossible to obtain a greater depth than 14 feet of water, because to have made the channel equal to the natural one, and of only 14 feet deep the expense would have been upwards of £400,000. Mr. Workman finds pleasure in detracting from those public services, and would do his best, even by assertions which he cannot sustain, to hold me up to public opprobrium ; nor does he hesitate to describe a work, unequalled in the world, and which he, as a citizen of Montreal, should be proud of, as "*Mr. Young's Lake St. Peter folly.*"

Against Mr. Workman's opinions, however, I have the great satisfaction of knowing, that the great majority of my fellow merchants have a full appreciation of my exertions in carrying forward to its present position the important work of perfecting the channel of navigation between the Ocean and Montreal. Believing that I am so supported, I shall be very slow to believe that any considerable number of my fellow citizens, in any section of the city, do sanction Mr. Workman's views in reference to my exertions for improving the navigation between Montreal and Quebec, nor have I any doubt, that some time or other, the importance of these exertions, in the growth and prosperity of Montreal as a sea and inland port, will be duly recognised and acknowledged.

It should be borne in mind that the expenditure on the Clyde, in Scotland, to the present time, to secure a channel from sea to Glasgow of twelve at low and eighteen feet at high water, has cost upwards of £2,000,000 sterling. To effect this about six million cubic yards of soil have been removed, while a twenty feet channel at low water will be secured to Montreal, by the removal of about five million cubic yards, at a cost not exceeding £190,000 !

Mr. Workman, with his usual inaccuracy, taunts me with having by my action thrown the burthen of this work on the trade of Montreal since 1845. Now, in the first place, the work

was not begun till 1850, and tonnage dues were first collected in 1852 ; and secondly it is a mistake to suppose that harbour or lake dues are paid by the city of Montreal alone. The people of Western Canada, who export flour, wheat, &c., or import merchandise for consumption, pay their proportion of harbour and lake dues as much as the people of Montreal, and are equally interested in every improvement, the tendency of which is to lessen these, and other charges in our port. Mr. Workman is quite right in saying that the improvement of the navigation below Montreal is as much a Provincial work as any canal, lock or lighthouse, from Burlington Bay to Belle Isle Straits. This view of the matter has for several years been represented to Government by the Harbour Commissioners, and the principle has been conceded, as I have before stated, by an advance from the Government on the plant of the Harbour Trust of £15,000 for the operations of this year, which is rather in contradiction to Mr. Workman's assertion that the "cost of the work," by the action of Mr. Young, "was thrown on the city of Montreal."

Mr. Workman may not be able "to repress a smile" at my *weakness* in supposing that a great "benefit" has been conferred on the city and trade of Montreal, by so improving the navigation, as to enable the largest vessels to ascend from sea instead of stopping at Quebec. This is Mr. Workman's affair. He may smile if he pleases, but he should not try to solace himself with the belief that every "sane" merchant coincides in his opinion. Mr. Workman assumes to speak for the body of merchants—he does speak as if he were their accredited organ ; but gives no kind of proof that he is so. For my own part I should believe that Mr. Workman has exhibited some of the "vanity," "absurdity" and "folly" which he so liberally attributes to me, rather than believe that the intelligent merchants of Montreal would look upon the Lake St. Peter improvement as a "folly," or approve of Mr. Workman's views in respect of it.

Mr. Workman, on a cool review of the whole subject, irrespective of personalities, will change his opinions on this point. When he does, he will be better able to appreciate the anxiety and labour which, as Chairman of the Harbour Commissioners, the accomplishment of this great result has cost me, not only in the arrangements with Government, but in carrying on so large and extensive a work, for so long a time without

Government aid or security, and in placing the credit of the Harbour Trust in a position only inferior to that of the Government Securities themselves.

I will now allude to Mr. Workman's criticism of a paragraph in my former letter, in which I ventured to take some credit to myself for having, in 1846, suggested the practicability and necessity of *a bridge across the St. Lawrence, a little below Nuns Island.* Mr. Workman is amazed at my presumption. He says " that " there is abundant evidence to prove that long " before I dreamt of such a structure, *or was* " *even much known amongst us,* it had been pub-" licly urged in the press and the suitability of " various points enlarged and dwelt upon.

" One correspondent of a Montreal journal " suggested a tunnel from Craig Street to St. " Lambert, while others urged the merits of an " iron suspension bridge, from the high bank " below the barracks to the Island of St. Helens, " of sufficient altitude to allow vessels to pass un-" der, whilst others suggested plans of a super-" structure of wood, with stone piers;—various " sites between Lachine and Boucherville were " pointed out as suitable termini on the south " side of the St. Lawrence. This was in the " interval between 1830 and 1842."

The point to be determined, is not whether correspondents had made mention, through the press, of a bridge over or under the St. Lawrence, previous to 1846. Mr. Workman *says* there was such correspondence—but that is not the question. The question is, was the present site for the bridge ever pointed out previous to the article of June 1846, published in the *Economist.* If it was, then I am wrong in supposing that I was the first to suggest that site; and if Mr. Workman will point out the correspondence, I shall admit my error frankly, and not trouble the public more about it. In the mean time, I take the liberty of reprinting a part of the article from the *Economist:*—

" Why should we go to the expense of building warehouses on the other side of the river if this can be avoided? But how is the difficulty to be overcome? We reply, by building a bridge across the St. Lawrence. This is no visionary scheme; we speak advisedly when we say it is perfectly practicable. Such a bridge can be erected from this side, a little below Nun's Island, at which part of the river the water is compara-tively shallow, and the shoving of the ice no-thing like so violent as lower down the river. By means of this bridge, we should have a con-stant access to the opposite shore, to the great convenience of trade. The freight and passen-ger cars could by this means run to a basin in the Canal for the special use of vessels loaded for the railroad. Such a bridge, it might be said, would obstruct navigation, but masted vessels with cargo would prefer the Canal, and for steamers, a hinge on the funnel could be made, as on the Rhine, and Seine in France, by which means the passage could be easily made. Such a scheme would at once do away with the necessity of building wharves and ferry boats, and of taking over property in winter on the ice," &c.

The suggestion in this article has become a fixed fact—the absurd tunnels and iron suspen-sion bridges, which Mr. Workman refers to are mere " folly" and unsubstantial " Will o' the wisps," which it suited Mr. Workman to bring up, leaving entirely out of view the real point for which I claimed credit. Again, even if I am not entitled to credit on that head, as having pro-posed the site, Mr. Workman knows well, cer-tain facts which might have induced him to spare his sneers, at my efforts in behalf of the bridge; that the survey of the bridge was car-ried on *by* my motion, as one of the Directors of the St. Lawrence and Atlantic Railroad in 1846, —that the surveys were made with funds ob-tained on my personal responsibility, and on funds advanced to a large extent by me, and only recently repaid under the Act for Bridging the St. Lawrence—that the result of the public meeting in 1846, and the surveys by Mr. Morton in 1846, of Mr. Gay in 1847, and of Mr. Gzowski in 1849, were largely instrumental in keeping the matter before the public, and all this before the survey made by Mr. Keefer in 1851. Mr. Workman is as usual in error in stating that the practicability of erecting the bridge at a point a little below Nuns Island, had not been shewn previous to Mr. Keefer's survey and report. Mr. Keefer's survey, and very able report, put the subject of the bridge first fairly before the pub-lic in Canada, and contributed largely to its being carried out. The immediate reason which led to the conveyance of the rights of the Mont-real and Kingston Railway to the Grand Trunk Company on the condition of their undertaking the bridge, has already been laid before the pub-lic. The condition was suggested by me when I was acting as Chief Commissioner of Public Works, and was accepted by the Hon. L. H. Hol-ton, who was then President of the Montreal and Kingston Railroad Company. Whether any, and if any, what degree of credit, I was en-titled to, for what I did in connection with the bridge, I now leave it to the public to judge.

Mr. Workman chooses to leave the real topics

of discussion, which were as to the best site for docks,—the best route for Western produce from the West—the necessity or not of a canal to connect the St. Lawrence with Lake Champlain, and to attach himself to personalities as of the greater importance. I have shewn so many examples of this, that there can be no difficulty in seeing how very far Mr. Workman has been drawn in this direction. Another example I will furnish before leaving the matter. Towards the conclusion of his letters he says, "he has no "public funds to spend in surveys, plans, and "printing in support of my views, no evidence "to quote from parties whose tenure of office "may be at my bidding." Mr. Workman excels in calling names, but he is no less able at throwing out insinuations. He, Mr. Workman, has no public funds to misappropriate, he has no screws to put upon unwilling officials, to squeeze out falsehood in support of his opinions; but it seems I have. Mr. Workman does not say so, but wishes the inference to be drawn. Now, if Mr. Workman is aware of any facts in support of his insinuation, it was his duty to publish them, and then to have denounced openly the misapplication of public funds, or the intimidation of officials for private or personal purposes or interests. If he has no facts, it would have been but simple justice to myself to have spared so wretched an insinuation.

In the expectation of being able to close this correspondence in my next letter, I am,

Your obedient servant,

JOHN YOUNG.

Montreal, Aug. 8th, 1859.

LETTER NO. 11.

To the Editor of the MONTREAL GAZETTE:

I have not heretofore nor do I intend to make an exception to the rule, of not answering anonymous correspondents, unless by a brief notice of some remarks made by your correspondent "A Constant Reader" in your journal of the 23d ult., wherein I am accused of an attempt to "hoodwink" your readers and of "misrepresenting" Mr. Workman as to the effect of the Navigation Laws of the United States, and as to the effect of cheaper inland freight on our foreign trade.

In reference to this matter I may state that my remarks on the actual working of the Navigation Laws of the United States in Canada, were the result of actual transactions frequently repeated in my own business. Mr. Wilson, the Vice-President of the Board of Trade, referred to by "A Constant Reader" in the extract published from a debate in the House of Commons, says that "he did not contend that the United States "were not technically right in their interpreta- "tion because by the law of 1817 the coasting- "trade was declared to be the trade from one "port in the United States to another." This corresponds exactly with what I stated, and what every business man knows to be the working of the law in Canada. Yet, "A Constant Reader" seems to endorse Mr. Workman's opinion that "the Navigation Laws of the United States "would alone be sufficient to prevent our ever "getting any portion of the Western trade." I simply pointed out the fact that a British vessel could load at any British port and sail direct to Whitehall or any other American port—and that a British ship could also load at Chicago and discharge at Montreal or any other Canadian port.

I will go further and state, that it would be quite in accordance with the Navigation Laws of the United States for a British vessel not only to load American produce at Chicago and discharge at Montreal, but it would also be legal for the same or any other vessel to reload the same produce, and clear from Montreal to any port in the United States. There is no relaxation of the Navigation Laws of the United States necessary to secure this—nor did I ever say there was. I only said in reference to the navigation of the Hudson River and of the New York Canals, that "I did not believe that the State of New York would refuse the free navigation of these canals to our vessels for the same right granted to New York craft for through freight, nor that the General Government of the United States would refuse us the right to navigate the Hudson, if in doing so the vessel were bound direct from a Canadian to an American port." In proof that this would probably be the case, I may state, that on the opening of the St. Lawrence Canals in 1849, I loaded the propeller "Ireland," with a general cargo direct for Chicago. This was the first vessel which had loaded at Montreal direct for Chicago, and was also the first vessel which loaded at Chicago and sailed direct for Montreal with cargo. British vessels, however, had then no right to navigate Lake Michigan any more than they have now the right to navigate the Hudson. That lake being wholly within the territory of the United States, British vessels could have been excluded; yet, it was not done, and such are the advantages of reciprocal trade to both countries that there can be little doubt, that the freedom of the Ottawa navigation will be deemed a fair equivalent for that of the Hudson, nor will the Navigation Laws of either country be thereby interfered with for the through voyage. "'A Constant Reader' says that it is not "cheapening inland freight to Montreal that Mr "Workman objects to, but to New York, its "great competitor. It is the cheapening of "freights to and from the United States Atlan. "tic ports at the expense of the St. Lawrence he "deems likely to be disastrous to our own "trade." This is exactly what I desired to prevent by the construction of the Caughnawaga Canal. It is because of the superiority and cheapness *now* of freights "to and from the United States Atlantic ports," through American routes, that the Canal into Lake Champlain has become so imperatively necessary, and also because *the experience* of the present system of things has proved "to be disastrous to our own trade." Mr. Workman and "A Constant Reader" do not object to the construction of the Welland Canal. But, is it not a matter too apparent for argument that, if the Welland Canal alone were constructed, and no other outlet provided *below Lake Ontario* than what now exists, " the cheap-"ening of freights to and from the United States. "Atlantic ports," so much dreaded by "A Constant Reader" and Mr. Workman, would thereby be still more cheapened ; and is it not clear, that if we are unable to compete successfully now for the Western trade with the Eastern States, it is evident we would be still less able to do so when freights were further cheapened, through the Oswego and other routes, by the enlargement of the Welland Canal, and without any increase to our power of competition beyond "our two excellent railways." It is this very "cheapen-"ing of freights to "New York, our great com-"petitor, at the expense of the St. Lawrence," which so loudly calls for the construction of a work by which Montreal and the St. Lawrence may get a share of the trade which *now* passes by her, and which would be more effectually secured to American routes than at present, if the Welland Canal alone was enlarged without an outlet on the Lower St. Lawrence being also provided.

It is also to place Montreal in a position to compete with New York, for *the foreign trade* (by which Mr. Workman means our exports by sea) and the trade of the Eastern States, that I advocate the construction of a canal into Lake Cham-plain, and not as "A Constant Reader" says, to put New York on the same footing as ourselves and to "destroy our advantage and ruin our foreign trade."

Now, one would suppose, from the frequent allusion by Mr. Workman and "A Constant Reader," to the *destruction* of our export or foreign trade by sea, that this trade was in a highly flourishing condition, and that our advantages were so great that it would be impoli-i-ic in the extreme to disturb such a delightful state of things. *It is because our export trade by sea is not at all satisfactory*, that I have urged upon my fellow-citizens and the public the adoption of measures calculated to produce a change. Mr. Workman and "A Constant Reader" may not be aware of the fact, that, while the exports of the Western States and of Western Canada have enormously increased during the last ten years, *the exports by sea from Montreal have decreased.* There is no disguising this fact, which the following table only makes too apparent :—

EXPORTS FROM MONTREAL BY SEA.

	Flour, bbls.	Oatmeal, bbls.	Pease, bush.	Wheat, bush.	Total in bushels.
1845	442,228	1,570	230,912	396,252	2,836,154
1846	556,692	5,030	216,340	534,717	3,558,906
1847	651,030	21,490	119,252	628,021	4,112,418
Average					3,502,492
1856	193,731	4,820	218,116	774,157	2,004,018
1857	239,501	292	196,418	854,912	1,244,495
1858	107,742	1,582	423,018	669,211	2,097,879
Average of last 3 years					2,114,134

Let it be borne in mind that the exports in 1845, 1846, and 1847 were greater than in any previous years, and also that they preceded 1848 —when for the first time the United States, by the Bonding, or Warehousing, Bill, admitted the products of Western Canada, to pass through the United States *in bond.* Previous to 1849, no exports from Western Canada *could be made* to the United States. In that year, shipments from Western Canada through the United States to Great Britain were commenced, and from that time to the present, the question of routes has merely been one of cost of transport. The superiority of the route *via* Oswego, may be estimated by the fact that the average exports of flour and grain from Canada West to the United States for 1856, 1857, and 1858, was equal to 5,556,670 bushels, being nearly three times greater than the whole exports by sea from Montreal, against no exports in 1848, and only 124,600 bushels in 1849. These figures conclusively shew, that what Mr. Workman and the "Constant Reader" call a foreign export trade from Montreal, has in ten years *decreased forty per cent,*—while in the same period the State of New York has gained a trade from Canada West, in flour and grain alone, averaging for the three years ending with 1858, of 5,556,070 bushels. Yet, "a Constant Reader" joins with Mr. Workman in whining about "*destroying our advantages, and ruining our foreign trade,*" when these gentlemen ought to be aware that our export trade from Montreal by sea, is not only not keeping pace with the progress of Western Canada and the Western States, or of the Atlantic U. States ports, but is actually less by forty per cent. than the average of the three years ending with 1847. These are, no doubt, disagreeable facts, but it Mr. Workman or "a Constant Reader" cannot contradict them, then I contend that their cry as to "our foreign trade being ruined, is only applicable to the present system of things, under which Western trade finds a cheaper outlet through American ports on Lakes Erie and Ontario, and can have no reference to those projects advocated by me, which the highest authorities assert *will secure* for the lower St Lawrence a share of that ever increasing interior trade, but which, as I have shewn, now passes from us through American routes from Lake Ontario.

I have not thought it worth while to allude to "A Constant Reader's" charge against me, for inconsistency in reference to my estimate of the transport of heavy freight by railroad being 1½ cents per ton per mile. If "A Constant Reader" will again examine my remarks on this subject, he will find that I stated that this rate at least, was necessary to provide against actual loss. I assumed this rate as a means of comparison, with the rates of transport by water, knowing that no one would attempt to contradict it, and in order to give the railway the greatest possible advantage in the comparison ; but while I did this, I was at the same time aware, that the official returns of the State of New York shewed that the average cost of moving freight by the "New York Central" and the New York and Erie Railroads, in 1856, 1857 and 1858, was 2 66-100 cents per ton per mile.

In closing this correspondence, on the comparative merits of the St. Lawrence with other routes from the West, and on Docks at Montreal, I may say, with Mr. Workman, "that "there are still a number of matters unnoticed "which at some future period may claim my "attention." In my previous letters I have avoided, as far as possible, giving my own opinions of the probable future of our trade, and have supported the views expressed in my letter of 10th December, by facts and figures taken from official sources, as well as public documents emanating from the merchants of this, the largest commercial city in British America, from Engineers the most eminent in their profession, and from the highest officers in the Government of the country. It remains for Mr. Workman, or other gentlemen, to impeach the correctness of the opinions expressed in these various documents, as to the necessity of the enlargement of the Welland and the construction of the Caughnawaga Canal, and of Docks at Montreal, and also of the opinions so confidently expressed of a vast increase to the trade on Canadian canals and railways, and of our city, which would follow the construction of those works. The discussion of subjects of such general public interest cannot fail, if properly conducted, to be advantageous and useful.

How far Mr. Workman has succeeded in his letters in placing "in their true aspect the wild projects advocated by Mr. Young," the public will now be better able to judge. It must be evident to Mr. Workman himself, that these wild projects, both as to canals and railways, Lake St. Peter and Dock improvements, have been mainly supported by a great majority of Mr. Workman's fellow merchants, and, I think are also supported by a great majority of the citizens of Montreal ; at all events they are supported by the frequently repeated opinions of every officer and engineer in the Government service, as well as by every other engineer who has yet been called upon for an expression of opinion ; always excepting Mr. Trautwine.

Leaving now the discussion of Mr. Workman's letters, I am tempted to transgress a little further on your space, and on the patience of your readers by bringing together a few of the important views to which I have had occasion to advert during the several discussions of the Public Works referred to ; but as your columns will be sufficient'y occupied by what I have already written, I shall conclude my further remarks in another letter. and am now,

Your obedient servant,

JOHN YOUNG.

Montreal, August 22nd, 1859.

To the Editor of the MONTREAL GAZETTE :

SIR,—The results and opinions to which I have been led in my previous letters, on the subject of the advantages which the St. Lawrence route from the West to the Ocean and to the Eastern States possesses in comparison with other routes through the United States, and in reference to the facilities for trade and manufactures which may be created at the Port of Montreal, may be summed up as follows :—

1st. That no adequate means of transport at present exist or will exist in Lower Canada, even when the Victoria Bridge is completed, to compete in cheapness with the routes through the State of New York, from Lakes Ontario and Erie, for the trade of the Western States and Western Canada.

2nd. That without an enlargement of the Welland Canal, and the construction of a Canal into Lake Champlain, that trade must continue to flow as now through American channels, leaving our Canadian canals and railways comparatively deserted and consequently unremunerative, and an annual tax on the people of this country.

3rd. That the amount of interest which has now to be paid *annually*, and which has to be raised by duties on imports, on the money borrowed to build those canals and to aid the construction of railways, *exceeds two million, four hundred thousand dollars,* over and above all receipts from these works.

4th. That the interests of the canals and railways are almost identical, and the prosperity of each must add to the business of the other.

5th. That the completion of the Welland Canal and the construction of the Lake Champlain Canal from the St. Lawrence, of a size commensurate with the magnitude of the capabilities of the St. Lawrence navigation, would give a decided superiority to the route of the St. Lawrence over every or any route which it is possible to have through the State of New York between the Western States, Western Canada, and the Eastern States, and render highly remunerative those canals and railways which at present are unproductive, and an annual loss to the Province.

6th. That with the navigation so improved and perfected, as to make the St. Lawrence route, through Lake Champlain, the cheapest, quickest and best for the great and ever-increasing trade of the Eastern States from the West, the Port of Montreal from the vast water power at command for milling, and from the facilities for receiving and holding property, which could so easily be created, and from the fact that such property could be held here, either for shipment direct by ocean vessel or for distribution to the various Eastern States, can be made the greatest and most convenient interior depot for Western trade on this Continent, while it would rapidly rise in importance as a receiving and shipping port between England and other countries.

7th. That while the interests of the City of Montreal would be vastly promoted by the adoption of such a policy, a revenue would be obtained from these great public canals and railways, which, combined, do not at present attract more than nine to ten per cent. of that trade,—to secure which was the avowed object of their construction.

8th. That there is nothing in the Navigation or Trade Laws of the United States and Canada which can prevent the largest commerce between both countries, and as that route which offers the greatest facilities as to cost and rapidity must, in the nature of things, ultimately command the largest share of that commerce, there is every inducement to proceed as rapidly as possible with those works, by which alone such a result can be attained.

These points might be increased in number, but too much space has already been occupied in the discussion. I may add, however, that one of the main objects I have had in view has been to give prominence to the facts and arguments upon which my opinions are based, so as to invite public attention to the subject. If these opinions are discussed and criticised, I can have no reason to complain, for the more that they are discussed the more likely it is that truth will be arrived at in the end. The personal turn given by Mr. Workman to the discussion has rendered necessary allusion to points wholly unconnected with the real matters at issue. This is a matter of regret, for there is sufficient ground for difference in the subjects of discussion themselves. I would fain hope that Mr. Workman's example may not be followed in future discussions on these points. I refrain from giving a numerical list of the many statements which Mr. Workman, in his letters, has so recklessly made without proof or foundation, and which it has been my unpleasant duty to contradict. Mr. Workman's experience as a merchant, and especially his knowledge of Western trade is fully understood and appreciated here, but, it was because parties at a distance would not have the same means of judging, that I have at so much length dwelt on his letters of " A Merchant." I am quite aware of Mr. Workman's ability as a man of business and as a banker, still, when I find him in his learned Bank Reports advocating free trade in money and in his letters of " A Merchant " protesting against free trade in merchandise, it cannot be expected that I can respect his knowledge of Political Economy any more than his opinions on a branch of trade in which he has never been engaged.

Mr. Workman tells us, and I receive the information I must confess with some surprise, that of late years Europe has had " a succession of deficient harvests," which has afforded a market for our surplus cereals, and that very moderate supplies will be needed from us for some time to come, in consequence of purchases having been made in Europe for this country. Now our short supply of cereals from the crop of 1858 was only temporary, and the probability is, that the exports from this continent in the year 1860 will be greater than ever before, in contradiction to what Mr. Workman would wish to be believed, that my expectation of a great increase in our future trade is fallacious. Mr. Workman should remember that only a small part of the land in Canada or the Western States is yet under cultivation, and that the North Western region of British America has an area lying west of the 98th meridian and above the 43d parallel which is not inferior in size to the whole United States east of the Mississippi, and is perfectly adapted to the fullest occupation by cultivated nations. If this is borne in mind, and also the fact that a great trade must inevitably flow from the great valley of the Ottawa, it seems to me to show a want of foresight to doubt the future vast increase of our trade and the policy which should adapt itself to that future. The increase of trade in the last 25 years will fail in my opinion as a comparison with the probable increase of Western trade in the next 25 years, and, therefore, I think an examination of the subject will afford good grounds, even to the most cautious, for entering upon the construction of these works calculated to attract to Lower Canada a share of that vast trade which even now exists, but which flows past us and must continue to flow past us except the works recommended in these letters are constructed.

To the Government of this country, and indeed to all who earnestly desire to see British institutions perpetuated on this continent, it is of the greatest moment, to prevent the possibility of any unfavorable comparisons being justly made between British America and the United States. If it is seen that our canals, railways and material advancement do not keep pace with those interests in the American Republic, dissatisfaction and disaffection will gradually but surely grow, and the inferiority of our progress and position will be ascribed to political causes, instead of to our own want of energy and foresight in developing our great natural advantages. In this great contest of rivalry with the State of New York for the interior trade, it will not for one moment, I think, be admitted that the people of Canada are inferior in energy and enterprise to our neighbors on the other side of the line. But at present, from the absence of those works to which I have so frequently alluded, we, as Canadians, can have no opportunity for competition in the Western trade. Indeed, the prosp   of our being able to attract any large sh   ° that trade over our railroads or through   .anals, even when the Victoria Bridge is completed, is most unsatisfactory; and the responsibility of the Government of this country, considering the vast interests now involved and the disastrous results which must inevitably flow from a longer inaction as to these works, calculated to produce a change, is a very grave one. Believing as I do that the views I have endeavored to point out are sound, I have, as a Canadian, only done my duty in urging them on public attention.

I repeat that it depends entirely on the energy and enterprise of the merchants and residents in Lower Canada generally, and especially of Quebec and Montreal, to say, how much of that vast interior trade can be attracted to the St. Lawrence route, either for export to the Eastern States, or for shipment to Europe. Familiar as I am with all the various routes from the West to the ocean, by a long and active experience in the trade, and knowing all the advantages and capabilities of the different receiving points on the lakes and the Atlantic, I have no hesitation in stating that I know of none which possesses the extraordinary advantages which may be made available at Montreal, as a great *entrepot* for trade. With an unlimited water power at our command, with docks completed, and every facility therein for saving time and charges by machinery,—with a 20 foot channel to sea at lowest water, and with the Victoria Bridge affording an easy means at all seasons of the year for transport throughout New England, there is no place on the continent superior to it. *But none of these results are possible without the enlargement of the Welland and Caughnawnga canals, on a scale for vessels of at least 800 tons, and otherwise perfecting the navigation.* With these works carried out, Canada would be in a position of competing successfully with the State of New York for a share of that vast and ever increasing interior trade.

These improvements could not fail to give greater importance and power to B. America than possibly can be attained if the Lower St. Lawrence is to continue in its present inferior position as a means of transit. To myself, personally, it is matter of comparatively little moment, whether these views, which I have so long urged on public attention, shall be speedily carried into effect by the Government or not. But as every succeeding year only tends to impress me more and more with their truth, I cannot help thinking that, in view of the vast public and private interests now involved in our canals and railways, it will ere long be a matter of regret that the Government of Canada had not sooner taken action on a subject upon which there has been so much unanimity of mercantile and professional opinion.

Yours, very truly,

JOHN YOUNG.

Montreal, 25th August, 1859.